WORMWOOD MARRIAGE

B H Carter

Contents

INTRODUCTION

This book is written with the author's understanding that life is about a spiritual journey in an individual's personal and public life. This spiritual journey begins with events in our lives, meeting specific individuals, being at a particular place at an exact time, and seeing our lives move in different and unexpected directions.

The author believes there is good and evil in the world and that there is a heaven and a hell. The author believes one makes personal decisions based on one's lifestyle and choices and that one makes spiritual decisions daily that impact all areas of life.

It is sold with the understanding that the author is not engaged in rendering spiritual, emotional, or professional advice. The author asserts that all characters are fictional and any similarity to actual individuals is a coincidence and not to be construed as the author engaging in micro-scoping or categorizing character.

The author disclaims any liability, loss, or risk, personal or otherwise, incurred directly or indirectly from reading this book.

CONNECT WITH THE AUTHOR

Website: www.bhcarterauthor.com

Instagram: www.instagram.com/bh_carterauthor

Twitter: www.twitter.com/bh_carterauthor

Facebook: www.facebook.com/BHCarterMinstry

Email: barbara@bhcarterauthor.com

WORMWOOD STAR

"The name of the star is Wormwood. A third of the waters turned bitter, and many people died from the waters that had become bitter" Revelations 8:11 (NIV).

WHAT HAPPENED TO THE HONEYMOON

I picked up voices as I stepped into the living room.

Since watching television shows like Jerry Springer or Maury Povich was Scotty's most enjoyable activity, I assumed the voices came from the TV in the back. When I walked into the bedroom, no Scotty was visible or television playing. *I must be hearing things. I could have sworn that I heard voices.*

My hands went to my hips. "Satan, you're not messing with my mind. I bind you in the name of Jesus!" I mumbled under my breath as I searched for Scotty.

While I strolled back to the living room, Scotty's voice boomed clearly from the deck. I heard my new husband communicating with his dead daughter, "Charlessa, you can come back. You're daddy's girl, and I miss you very much. My psychic says you're resisting."

A hand went over my mouth, and I stepped back, my purse and keys dropping onto the sofa table. A spirit of fear and apprehension temporarily gripped me. My body trembled and my heart moved to my throat. Unable to budge, I stood motionless like a chunk of marble. I had been married to the man I now felt was Satan's son for four weeks before observing his bizarre behaviors.

I stated softly but boldly, "He who is in me is greater than he who is in the world."

I weighed my options. *Should I go out to the deck?*

*What if he **has** conjured up an evil spirit? Do I want to do spiritual warfare?*

Still posed like a chiseled statue, glaring toward the deck, spotting Scotty, my head spun, and I fell against the wall. We'd only been married for a month, and my new husband sat on our deck talking to a dead person. The shaking lessened, my heart rate settled, and I was able to move.

I had to think fast before he or his companion spirits sensed my presence. Should I confront or avoid it? Avoidance was painless, so I chose to leave. I picked up my purse and keys, stealthily tiptoed back to the front door, opened it without a screech, and slammed it shut loudly.

Galumph!

I re-entered, strolled into the living room, toward the dining room, and Scotty waved from the deck. I approached him, pecked his lips, and asked what he was doing.

"Nothing." His eyes twitched, and he slid a black book with gargoyles and upside-down crosses on the front cover into his pocket. "It was such a beautiful day that I decided to get some sunshine on the deck."

My arms crossed my chest. "I thought I heard voices coming from the deck," I said in my singsong voice.

A sideways glance from him caused my arms to drop to my sides, and my face tilted toward the wooden floor.

"You must be losing your mind, Hannah. As you can see, no one is out here but me, so you definitely didn't hear talking."

A close-lipped smile froze on my face. *I'm not going to start an argument. I know what I heard, and it was not in my mind.*

I decided to change the subject. "What do you want for dinner?" My eyes lifted to meet his gaze, wondering if my spirit would spot any evil in his eyes.

"I don't care." His shoulders shrugged. "Whatever you put together will be okay with me."

We ate silently after preparing a quick meal of broiled T-bone steaks, salads, and baked potatoes. Scotty scarcely communicated with me about his personal life since his daughter's death. Afterward, I rushed off to my second job at the school.

Unbeknownst to me, until his psychic called to reschedule an appointment, Scotty had resumed seeing her after Charlessa's death.

The only way I could find out what was happening in his life, which also affected my life, was to listen in on his conversations.

By eavesdropping, I discovered he saw her daily and participated in witchcraft and séances, trying to bring his daughter back.

After discovering that he was seeing a psychic, I read the eleventh chapter of Luke to him many times until he flatly told me he didn't want to hear them. Without causing him to say I thought I was a know-it-all, with humility and a soft voice, after reading the scriptures, I tried to show how he was opening himself up for more wicked imps to enter *his* spirit.

> *"When the unclean spirit is gone out of a man, he walketh through dry places, seeking rest; and finding none, he saith, I will return unto my house whence I came out. And when he cometh, he findeth it swept and*

garnished. Then goeth he, and taketh to him seven other spirits more wicked than himself; and they enter in, and dwell there: and the last state of the man is worse than the first" Luke 11: 24-26 (KJV).

The last time he listened to me explain the verses, he'd said, "I saw a psychic every day for twenty years when I was younger, and I'm no worse off for it. I stopped seeing her for many years because things were going well, and I didn't need her. I need her guidance now." He rolled his eyes. "My life seems to be turning to soot, and she is the only one who can help me get back on track. So, stop reading me those scriptures. I know the scriptures better than you do, so I don't need you trying to instruct me, okay?"

I thought, *Yeah, as Satan's son, you probably do know the scriptures better than I do—you just don't live them.* We studied the Bible together when we dated, and he enjoyed my interpretations. Now, Scotty said I was a hypocritical Christian, so obviously, he wouldn't receive what I was trying to impart to him.

Scriptures from the gospel of Matthew and Luke came to mind. When the Spirit led Jesus into the wilderness to be tempted by the devil, Satan used the scriptures to try to tempt Jesus, so Satan knows the scriptures.

To add fuel to the fire brewing within our home, besides enjoying Springer and Povich, programs that appeared to degrade women, parading most as cheaters, adulterers, or gold-diggers, Scotty was also addicted to Crossing Over and Ghost Whisperer. These TV sites were shows that facilitated communications between the living and the dead, presenting the dead as still being among the living.

After the first incident of hearing Scotty talking to Charlessa, when I came home early, he conversed with her multiple times as if she was still alive. He spoke to her in the hallway, on the deck, but mostly in our bedroom. Scotty spent most of his time isolated. He ate, slept, and spent his day locked away in the bedroom, if not at his medical equipment and transportation business. He even gave up all of his board positions but one.

More familiar spirits attached themselves to Scotty after he opened the door through psychic involvement and witchcraft. He was destroying himself and his life by dabbling in the occult, but he wouldn't listen to our pastors or me. As his wife, I felt obligated to remind him what our pastor and many other preachers said happens when we open our spiritual door for demonic spirits to enter. Of course, my words fell on deaf ears.

Still obsessed with killing Lenny, the man Scotty thought was sleeping with me, he was even more fixated on killing the man he thought was responsible for his daughter's death.

Dipping into his retirement funds, he hired a private investigator to discover everything about Charlessa's former boyfriend. He found that his name was Boston Matheson, but his cronies called him BM, for Boss Man and Big Man.

Boston turned out to be more notorious and higher ranking than Scotty expected. Having started as a Chicago gang leader, he had maneuvered his way into a respectable position. According to Scotty, Boston Matheson was a handsome, intelligent, charismatic drug dealer with a Master of Business Administration degree from Northwest-ern University. Wealthy adoptive parents had raised him; the Chicago media frequently connected their names to organized crime.

Sitting opposite Scotty as he studied the report, he mumbled as he re-read the file, "This picture doesn't look like the dude I saw her out with, and he don't look like no dealer. She must have been living with someone else."

My shoulders just shrugged because I had not met her boyfriend.

After studying Boston's picture for several days, Scotty said during dinner, "I may have seen Charlessa with this dude a few times, but she never said he was her boyfriend or that they were living together."

He took his glasses off and studied the photo. "Yeah, I think this is the same man I saw her shopping with."

His chin dropped to one shoulder; he said, "This dude lives in Chi-town, and Charlessa had an apartment in Madison."

His brows creased as he pinched the bridge of his nose.

"I'm gonna get to the bottom of this."

THE DEVIL'S MARRIAGE

Before marriage, I was joyful, energetic, and happy. Now I was sad, lethargic, and depressed most of the time. *Will I ever return to how I was before I married Scotty?* I wondered. What I went through with him before the marriage was utter madness. An evil spirit must have crept in and *possessed* me to marry him with all the mayhem and scurrility before our wedding.

Massaging my shoulders while tilting my ears toward my left and right shoulders, I walked to the tinted, stained-glass window on the front door. The tree branches swung in the wind, and I reflected on some conversations with Aunt Lucy. My memory recalled some of the words of wisdom she had given me when I cried to her about Scotty's jealousy. *That is spiritual warfare you're dealing with, baby. That old devil comes to steal, kill, and destroy. You've got to stay prayed up, Hannah. Satan leaves us for a season, but he returns with more attacks. All Christians are in spiritual warfare with the devil.*

> *"For we wrestle not against flesh and blood, but against principalities, against powers, against the rulers of the darkness of this world, against spiritual wickedness in high places"* Ephesians 6:12 (KJV).

I appreciated my aunt's wisdom and tried to follow her insights and revelations.

My attention turned to a couple strolling hand in hand, smiling and talking, and love seemed to emanate from them, something missing from our marriage. My view returned to the tree branches swinging in the wind, and I reflected on more of Aunt Lucy's wisdom. *One consolation for us Christians is that Satan's mode of operation has not changed; he tempts us just like he tempted Eve in the Garden of Eden with deception and lies. And even though we are in this spiritual battle, we are winners because we know our enemy's strategy and can defeat him with the Word of God.*

My eyes returned to the twosome and followed them until they turned the corner. I twisted my wedding ring, questioning why I waited until I was in my forties to make the inexplicable mistake of being used, abused, and mistreated by a man at a phase when I was more committed to the Lord and thought I *knew* the Lord's voice. I still refuse to admit that I actually married someone who got advice from a psychic. My shoulders slumped, and I buried my face in my hands.

I knew what II Corinthians 6:14 (KJV) stated,

> *"Be ye not unequally yoked together with unbelievers; for what fellowship hath righteousness and unright-*

eousness? And what communion hath light with dark-
ness?"

The Holy Spirit had presented signs to me multiple times that I was yoking with unrighteousness. Yes, Scotty was a believer, but he wasn't a righteous, faithful saint. I had to nudge him several times on Sunday mornings to keep him from snoring as I sat beside him in church.

He always replied, "I'm not sleeping. I'm listening to the pastor."

After service, he lectured *me* on what it meant to be a Christian, avoiding discussing his sleeping. "You don't have to do all that jumping and shouting to praise the Lord. Just because I don't run around the church like a madman doesn't mean I'm not saved." He exhaled with a moan.

"And just because I listen to the preacher with my eyes closed doesn't mean I'm sleeping."

I'd say, "That's true, but a person thankful for what the Lord has saved them from will raise their hands sometimes, or at least sing along with the praise and worship team as they praise and worship the King of Kings and Lord of Lords."

"I'm just as saved as you and anyone else at that church. I walk out doing Praise and Worship because they praise too long. It doesn't take all that to praise the Lord."

He didn't demonstrate any of the fruits of the Spirit – love, joy, peace, patience, kindness, goodness, faithfulness, gentleness, and self-control found in Galatians 5:22-23. He professed to be a Christian, and I stubbornly and arrogantly refused to look at his fruits.

I quickly read past Matthew 15:7-8 (KJV),

> *"Ye hypocrites, well did Esaias prophesy of you saying,*
> *This people draweth nigh unto me with their mouth,*
> *and honoureth me with their lips; but their heart is far*
> *from me."*

This doesn't pertain to Scotty and me. Jesus was speaking to the Scribes and Pharisees of His day. So, I shrugged off the Word of God rather than embracing it.

Scotty talked the religious talk, but he didn't walk the walk. He didn't have Jesus in his heart. He deceived me, as well as many other Christians, with his holy and religious conversations. If hypocrisy happened when Jesus lived on the earth, it certainly would happen during my lifetime. I had been in church most of my life and understood that people went to church for various reasons, and many of those reasons were not to worship, praise, and honor Jesus.

In retrospect, I think I wasn't even totally submitted. I didn't want to admit that I had disobeyed the Holy Spirit and married an unrighteous man. So, I kept telling myself that *Scotty* needed to study the Bible and submit to Jehovah.

I wouldn't admit that Scotty went to church; yes, but the church wasn't in him. I wouldn't admit that Scotty had a *spirit* of religion, but he was not spiritual, meaning he didn't serve the Father (our God), Jesus (God's Son), and Holy Spirit (our Teacher). Scotty knew the talk and the jargon. My spouse knew what to say to make churchgoers think he was a spirit-filled man. But he was not filled with the Holy Spirit that Jesus said would endue us with power from on high.

*"And, behold, I send you the promise of my Father upon
you: but tarry ye in the city of Jerusalem, until ye be
endued with power from on high"* Luke 24: 49 (KJV).

The devil arranged our marriage, figuratively speaking.

There was no consummation of our marriage. There was no, *"And
Scotty knew Hannah, his wife"* on our wedding night or during the
marriage's tenure. The first book of the Bible talks about consummat-
ing a marriage.

*"And Adam knew Eve his wife; and she conceived, and
bare Cain"* Genesis 4:1 (KJV).

I was not hoping to conceive and bear a child, but I did expect
that as husband and wife, we would have *known* each other for at least
some time during the marriage. We committed fornication before our
union, and he had no problems performing. We kept our vows to wait
until we were married to be sexually intimate again. Biblically, we now
had the right to know each other as husband and wife without breaking our covenant with Yahweh. But there was no hugging, cuddling,
kissing, intimacy, or sex after we said, "I do." Our marriage began
without affection, touching, or communication, along with mistrust,
jealousy, and accusations of infidelity.

Scotty continued to make critical and negative comments about
me and continued with his condemnatory attitude and verbal abuse.
Months into the marriage, while searching through dresser drawers
and looking for blank checks, I discovered an entire bottle of Viagra
prescribed for Scotty. *This script must be an old prescription from when*

we slept together before marriage. To my dismay, the date on the bottle showed it was a current prescription.

Why would he have a prescription for Viagra, and he and I are not having sex? Is he sleeping with someone else? Is he denying me privileges as a wife yet sharing those privileges with someone not his wife? Questions raced through my mind, and my body didn't know whether to get angry or sad. My teeth clamped with anger as I headed to the kitchen to dump the pills. But then tears welled in my eyes, and my lips trembled as thoughts battered my head that I was a fool—pain shot through my temples. Pills still in my hand, I headed to the medicine cabinet to find aspirin, rubbing my temples.

After swallowing two aspirins and lying down for thirty minutes, I put the Viagra back in the drawer. I didn't think he'd ask me about them, but I knew he could quickly obtain another script.

As I strolled to the kitchen, I muttered, "Scotty manipulated and conned me before we were married. Why would I think it would change after marriage?"

Having a conversation with myself, I said, "But I didn't realize he was conning and manipulating me at the time."

My thoughts flashed back to our first year of courtship. Scotty stood in the doorway until I was safely in my car. He cleaned the snow off of my car before I went to work. Scotty limped in the rain or snow to bring the car and pick me up at the doorway so I wouldn't get wet. Where is the man peeping through the blinds or standing in the yard until I am safely in the house?

When you're caught up in Satan's ploys and yielding to your lustful desires, you don't see what is before your eyes. I discovered after marriage that Scotty had taken Viagra to seduce me. The con job was that he took Viagra before our union and stopped taking it after the wedding. That didn't make sense to me. You would think he would take an impotence drug after getting a wife so he could fulfill his marital duties as a husband.

That's why I said it was a con, and Scotty and his dad, Lucifer, set me up. My *husband* wasn't interested in sex with me, but he demonstrated his virility to reel me in. Sure, Scotty nor Satan forced me to caress Scotty, cuddle with him, or have sex with him, but Lucifer knew my desires and made them accessible to me. I believe Satan keeps a report card on us, putting an asterisk on what he knows tempts us easily. Like a lamb led to slaughter, I took the bait. I'm not saying I was guiltless because I wasn't an innocent lamb. I was just as guilty as Scotty.

Turning around before I took fish and vegetables from the freezer for dinner, I strolled back to the bedroom, stared at the pills in the bottle, and rolled the vial around in my hand. I sat on the floor crossed-legged, my mind going a mile a minute, trying to figure out what might be happening. My chest heaved as I reread the name and date on the bottle, hoping I had misread and it was a script for his brother.

After several minutes of massaging my temples and fighting back the tears, I realized I would not know what was happening unless I asked Scotty, which I would never do. He would accuse me of going through his stuff and spying on him, and then he'd tell me it was none of my business. I figured the most logical thing to do was to continue as I had for the past months.

After finding the pills, I sat at home alone and withdrawn after work for weeks, not wanting to talk to anyone. Avoidance and fleeing were much more manageable than confronting and fighting. Rather than discuss with Scotty or share my frustrations with a trusted friend, I ignored the situation praying it would work itself out. *What is going on in our relationship? What type of union do we have? What kind of marriage does a husband and wife not ever become intimate? Why does Scotty have a prescription for impotence tablets?* I asked myself.

I had prayed that things would get better between us after we married, the past was behind us, and Scotty had me as his wife. Instead, Scotty got worse and brought up things from the past daily. During our pre-marital counseling, I asked him to forgive me for everything I had done to cause *suspicion,* even though I had done nothing wrong. Our pastors had instructed us to repent of all misgivings, ask each other for forgiveness, bury the past, and start afresh with a clean slate. All of the things Scotty forgave me for he brought up daily.

"I know you're having an affair with that dude, Lenny."

"You lied about knowing the young man at the video store."

"You disrespected me by giving the doctor your telephone number in front of me."

"You embarrassed me by leaving me while we walked to the church when we were supposed to be together."

He resurrected everything that displeased him during the years we had dated.

I questioned the Holy Spirit. "Do I have to stay in this marriage? What does the Bible say about my situation?" I conjectured that I would have to study the Bible to discern what God said about our marital situation.

Depression crept close by because I feared *I* was failing in another marriage. Tears welled in my eyes five to six times a day whenever I thought of separation. I did not want a breakup or a divorce, although our marriage was not the union I had imagined either. I questioned why *I* couldn't salvage our relationship, why *I* couldn't improve our marriage through prayer, and why *I* was having problems in my marriage when *I* was a Christian and a good wife.

Satan whispered that I was such an awful person, a pitiful human being, and a failure because I couldn't keep a husband. What *was* wrong with me? *Why couldn't I keep a husband like other Christian women? Why did I always select the terrible men? What happened to the man who was to love, honor, respect, and protect me?* If this union ended in a breakup, it would be my second failed marriage. I wiped the tears creeping down my face with my fingers. Was I being punished for some past sins?

THE TRAIN TRIP

Approximately six weeks into our marriage, Scotty came home one evening and said we were going to New York.

"An associate of mine bought these train tickets for him and his wife to spend a four-day weekend in New York during the US Open Tennis Championship. He said they had an emergency and wouldn't be able to go. The man was going to give me the tickets, but I made him take a hundred bucks. He also gave me two tickets to the Yankees game. So start packing your bags because we'll leave at 6:00 p.m. this Thursday."

"6:00 Thursday? That sounds wonderful, Scotty, but I'm not sure if I can go. I'm scheduled to work at the hospital this weekend."

"Call in sick! I'm sure they can find someone else. We don't get opportunities like this every day. You need time away. You've been working very hard, and you're looking tattered."

I moved to a mirror to look at my face. *I'm not looking frazzled.* I yelled from the bathroom. "It would be fantastic to have four days off to relax and rest." A slow hum of anticipation crept from my mouth as I strolled back to the kitchen. "But I don't like to call in sick if I'm not. My stomach twists and churns when I lie." My lips twisted from side to side. "I'm sure I can find someone to switch weekends with me. It may mean I have to work two weekends in a row. But that's okay." A finger covered my lips as I thought. "It'll be worth spending four days in New York City. I'll visit another city on my bucket list."

Scotty smirked. "Suit yourself. I'm going whether you go or not." He paused for a second and then added mordantly. "You lie about everything else. I don't see why you feel funny when lying about being sick."

My lips clamped together to keep from saying anything. I pranced to the bedroom, shaking my head to a jingle on TV.

Fortunate to find someone to switch weekends with me at such short notice; Thursday evening, we boarded the train for New York City.

We changed trains in Chicago, boarding ahead of the non-dis-abled passengers because Scotty walked with a cane. While sitting and observing boarding passengers, a tall, handsome, dapperly dressed, professional-looking young man walked past us. Scotty jumped up abruptly, holding the back of the seat in front of him, knocking the book I was reading out of my hands. He leaned over me, his eyes following the young man.

I turned to see if Scotty was eyeing the younger, smaller man or the older, stockier one walking behind. Both men took seats in the train car behind us. "Do you know them, Scotty? They look very professional, like businessmen or business owners."

"Uh, hum. Well, I think I do. The younger one looks like Charlessa's old boyfriend, BM."

"BM?"

Scotty plopped back down in his seat. My skin crawled as the angry, hateful, vindictive, vengeful spirits emanated from Scotty. I ran my hands up and down my arms, attempting to dismiss the crawling feeling of ants.

"Boston Matheson," Scotty said, snarling.

After seeing the young man, Scotty couldn't sit still. He shifted in his seat, dropped his eyeglasses, knocked the book out of my hand again, and finally tried to read the newspaper. He couldn't concentrate; he peeped back at the man he thought was Boston Matheson every few minutes.

The young man walked past us again and trotted down the black spiral staircase to the sleeping accommodations. Scotty called for the car attendant and requested our sleeping berths close to Boston Matheson, saying he was a close friend. The attendant returned and informed us that no sleeping cars remained in car number sixteen, Mr. Matheson's car. But he could move us to number seventeen.

Scotty said, "Thanks, man," and slipped him a twenty-dollar bill.

Scotty had difficulty going up and down stairs, and the narrow spiral staircase was tricky for him to navigate. But he was determined, and we moved at a snail's pace to our sleeping berths.

With the door to our roomette open, Scotty stretched his neck like a rooster, glancing back to Boston's car every few minutes. Around 5 p.m., Scotty's body tightened as he studied car number sixteen. I stepped into the corridor to see what caused his distress. The young man and another well-dressed man strolled past me, said hello, and climbed the stairs toward the upper level of the train.

Scotty used the door frame to pull up to a standing position. "Let's go eat in the dining room upstairs."

"Why don't we have the car attendant bring our meals to us, and you don't have to struggle climbing up and down those narrow stairs."

He headed for the same staircase Mr. Matheson had used. When he started up the stairs, he handed me his cane and used both hands to grab the railings to pull up each rung as he struggled up the curved stairs. From our berth to the dining car, Scotty pulled and dragged, held the rail with his left hand, and used his right hand to pull his right leg up. Sweat drenched his face as he strained to steer the spiral staircase to the dining area and Boston Matheson. Five minutes later, flushed and sweat dripping from his face to his shirt, he finally dragged his right leg up the last rung.

He stopped to catch his breath, pointing to an empty table. "Grab me a couple of napkins from that table."

As requested, I gave him a hand full of white paper napkins. He wiped the sweat off his face, stood up as straight as possible, squared his shoulders, and raised his chin high, adjusting his clothing. He pasted a slight closed-lipped smile and asked the waiter if he could be seated at the table with BM, facing closest to the TV because he wanted to watch the game.

We sat opposite BM and the well-dressed gentleman next to him. With a slightly tucked chin and enigmatic smile, Scotty said, "I'm Scotty, and this is my wife, Hannah. How are those Cubs doing? The Cubs have always been my favorite baseball team. I guess because I spent much time in Chicago when I was younger."

BM didn't lift an eye and continued whispering to the older, conservatively dressed man next to him, wearing a navy suit and starched, white shirt with a navy and red necktie. Neither of them acknowledged or responded to Scotty's comments.

Scotty smiled to the side. "I'm sorry. That was rude of me to interrupt your conversation like that. We'll just sit here and catch the game. This spot was the only open area near a television."

BM's eyes rolled up to check who was determined to disrupt his conversation. His lips pressed together, he scanned Scotty from his head to his folded hands on the table and resumed discussing without addressing him.

I went to the counter and ordered our food, and Scotty and I watched the game until our food arrived.

After several minutes, the two men stood and walked toward the snack bar.

The friend went through the doors into another car, but BM sauntered back to our table, gave us a broad smile, and apologized. "I'm sorry if I was rude a few minutes ago. I had to finish up a business matter. I'm Boston, but I prefer to be called BM. Would you two like a cocktail to go with your dinner?"

"We're fine with coffee," said Scotty. "Have a seat. I want to know what's been happening in the game."

BM brought Scotty current during the commercials, telling him all of the prior actions, fouls, and magnificent batting that had happened before we sat down.

Scotty knew how to be charming and kind when it benefited him. He enamored BM, laughing, telling sports jokes, and never telling him he was Charlessa's dad. Without emotion, he discussed a young lady's drug-related, execution-style death a few months back in Madison, WI. "Her name was Charlessa Brian." Scotty paused to study BM's reaction.

BM was cool as a cucumber and calm as the east wind.

He didn't share any knowledge of the incident or acknowledge knowing Charlessa.

"It was all over the news." Scotty's head tilted. "Say, are you from Chi-town or Wisconsin?"

"Born and raised in Chicago. Where are you two from?" He flashed a million-dollar smile at me.

"We're from Madison, Wisconsin. Have you ever been there?" asked Scotty.

"I can't say that I have. I thought Madison was a college town with cheeseheads and beer drinkers." He winked at me, and my chin dropped to my chest. "I've never been to Madison." He clamped his lips with two fingers covering his mouth and his thumb underneath his chin with a faraway look in his eyes. He smiled at Scotty. "But I don't think I've missed anything exciting."

I thought, *now, we will argue about me flirting with this man young enough to be my son because he winked at me. BM is just being friendly, but Scotty takes everything the wrong way.*

I sensed Scotty's body tense, his countenance darken, and a demonic silhouette growing more extensive the redder and redder he became listening to BM talk about never being in Madison and not acknowledging that he knew Scotty's precious Charlessa.

Under the table, Scotty's fists clenched. He forced a tight-lipped smile as he and BM conversed. BM talked about a jazz club he owned with pride.

I caught myself staring at Boston Matheson as he talked. I found it hard to believe that the handsome, clean-cut, intelligent, educated young man sitting opposite me could be a drug dealer. He stood about 6 feet 3 inches tall, weighed about 180 pounds, and had a short military-style haircut. Perfect straight, white teeth glistened when he smiled. His parents must have spent thousands on dental work. He had the most beautiful smile I had ever seen. He was clean-shaven, in excellent physical shape, and had a physique like a running back, boxer, and point guard.

Saliva pooled in my mouth as I studied the handsome man, and I swallowed hard. I understood why Charlessa was attracted to BM. I wondered if Scotty had the right man. This guy didn't talk, act, or look like a big-time drug dealer.

Scotty tried to sneak in a casual question about BM's business. "So, BM, what type of work do you do? You look like you might be a young business owner."

"You've got good intuition, Mr. Scotty. I am a small business owner. I told you about my jazz club. I'm also in the interstate trucking business."

When Scotty asked about his trucking business, Boston pulled business cards out for his jazz club and trucking operation and handed them to Scotty and me. "If you're ever on the south side, stop by, and we'll treat you like royalty."

"When did you start the trucking business, and how long have you been doing it?"

BM sat up straight. "You ask a lot of questions for someone I just met. Are you this nosey with everyone that you meet?" He peered into Scotty's eyes.

Scotty flashed a broad smile and mimicked BM's body language. "Hey, BM, I didn't mean to ruffle your collar. I'm just trying to be friendly."

BM stood, smiled slyly at Scotty, and winked at me. "I'll talk to you later, old man, and you take care, Mrs. Scotty." He tapped Scotty gently on the shoulder as he walked away.

Scotty opened his mouth to respond, but BM moved swiftly out of our sight, two line-backer-built men walking behind him. "He is one arrogant prick! I wanted to kick his butt, but it's not time yet." He growled. "Who does he think he is dismissing me like I'm a child!?" He ripped the business cards and threw them on the floor.

I smiled and glanced at the television. *Scotty has met someone as arrogant as him and someone who's not intimidated by his domineering, aggressive behavior.*

"What are you smiling at? What's funny?"

"Some of the things sports players do are funny to me, and some things that men do make me laugh."

Scotty looked at me like I was speaking a foreign language, mumbled something under his breath, and stood up. "Let's go back to our berth!"

The following morning, after seeing BM and his companions saunter past us and swiftly climb the stairs to the dining car, Scotty struggled up the stairs for breakfast.

He was hoping to find out BM's destination by befriending him; still fixated on getting revenge for the death of Charlessa. Scotty felt BM was the reason for his daughter's untimely and violent death. He wouldn't accept that she chose to date BM and had lived with him for nearly two years. According to her mother, BM paid for Charlessa's condo in Madison and split his time between Chicago and Madison. She must have had some inkling of his profession. Charlessa was probably attracted to him and stayed with him because he was handsome, intelligent, and rich.

Scotty limped over to the table with his cane where BM was eating breakfast and teased him about his big breakfast.

"You don't look like you would eat that much, man. I guess it must all go to your feet."

BM smiled. "Why don't you two join me, and I can watch how much you eat, old man. Good morning, Mrs. Scotty. Did you sleep well last night?"

I opened my mouth to tell him my last name was Brian, or he could call me Hannah, but Scotty interjected. "Where do you get off?

Hannah and I are going to New York City, where nobody sleeps." He'd said he hoped to find out BM's destination, exit at the same stop, and wait for an opportunity when BM was alone to shoot or stab him.

Having a criminal mind and a gangster personality, Scotty was skilled at smuggling weapons on his person when we traveled. He always had a knife; most of the time, he also had a small, twenty-two-caliber pistol. I still can't quite explain how Scotty taped the blade. When security systems at the airports and train stations went off, Scotty showed the medical report from his physician that he had pins in his hips and knees. He carried the statement whenever we traveled to prevent us from being delayed. I'm unsure how he smuggled the pistol past security, but he did on many occasions.

BM didn't answer, chewed, and swallowed the food.

"So, Mr. Scotty, will you buy up New York for Mrs. Scotty?"

Before Scotty could respond, the well-dressed gentleman who ate dinner with Boston walked to the table and nodded at BM. Boston wiped his mouth with a napkin, drank the rest of his apple juice, and stood up. "You all enjoy your trip to New York."

Scotty was so furious the veins in his neck enlarged. He had missed out on this opportunity and didn't know if he would get another chance to kill BM. We sat in silence during breakfast. Then, Scotty's face lit up. "He told us some of the things he liked to do last night and mentioned some club he owns in Chicago. Where's that card that he gave you last night, Hannah?"

"Didn't he give you one too?" I said in a fruity voice, knowing he had thrown them on the floor last night.

Scotty's shoulders slumped as he waited for me to find the cards.

I retrieved the cards from my purse and gave both to Scotty. Scotty read the information on the cards, pulled his wallet out, and carefully filed the cards in the charge card holder section.

We didn't spot BM again and weren't sure if he changed cars or got off at one of the stops.

While in New York, we went to four Broadway plays, catching day and evening performances and buying tickets from people on the streets or at the half-price ticket kiosk.

For the Yankees game, we had excellent seats behind home plate. Scotty feigned illness, and we missed the tennis championships. It was a beautiful, relaxing time for me.

Scotty was his old charming self that weekend, with only a few incidents of yelling. Because he ultimately did something to upset me, and I didn't want the trip ruined, as most of our trips, I went out of my way to be accommodating and agreeable. I ignored whatever he did to irritate or embarrass me while we were in New York. I didn't know anyone, so when he joked about me at the restaurants, yelled at me in the hotel, or called me names in the taxi, I didn't let it wreck my trip.

JOURNAL REVELATIONS

When Scotty recovered at my home before we married, he read my diary and my most intimate and personal thoughts and swore he would read it again. Fearing he would find my new journal and read it, I was leery of writing my inner thoughts and deepest feelings.

After attending a women's faith conference, the speaker urged us to try journaling for one month. The Evangelist reiterated that journaling was an excellent way to decrease stress and deal with emotional issues; it could also be a good cleansing for the soul. "You ladies should also consider starting a prayer journal." She smiled as she gazed over the attendees. "How else will you know if God has answered your prayers?"

She pointed to a PowerPoint slide on a whiteboard.

"Turn to the back of your manual, and you'll find blank pages." She fiddled with papers on the podium while waiting for us to locate the pages. "I'll show you how to design it." A red light hit the screen as a laser pointer focused on a diagram with four headings. "Make four columns and label each as you see on the diagram, Prayer Requests, Thanksgiving, Answered Prayers, and Thanksgiving."

Another screen glided onto the whiteboard with handwriting underneath the four headings. "These are examples of my prayer requests for the past year." Her smile seemed to reach her ears. "All of my prayers were granted. You see thanksgiving twice because you believe God answered you on your first ask, and you thank Him. When you receive your request, you offer thanksgiving to Yahweh again."

Her arms crossed her chest. "Does this make sense?"

Several hands went up with questions and comments. The Evangelist responded positively to negative responses and pleaded with the women to try it for a month.

After the conference, I rushed home excited and inspired to give journaling another try. I couldn't wait to start my prayer journal. The preacher's words made sense. How would I know if my prayers were answered if I didn't keep a journal of answered prayers? If my prayers were answered, the journal would help me remember the requests and God's responses. It would visually demonstrate that Jehovah cared for me.

After dinner, I sat on the toilet, my new diary on my lap, and tried to write. My mind went blank, and the pen didn't move. Thoughts of Scotty questioning me about journal notes he'd read scrolled through my head. A deep sigh crept from my lips. I tucked the notebook under my blouse, went to the second bedroom, and hid it in a purse.

The next night, I tried again to write and could not resume jotting my emotions on paper. After several nights of praying and attempting to journal, I finally wrote a feeling. The Holy Spirit then prompted me to read my past diary notes, whispering, "You should study your journal to see if you have grown spiritually."

During breaks from my jobs, I read my diary, from when I met Scotty to our wedding day. No signs of spiritual growth flashed, but my relationship's pandemonium and mayhem blazed like the midday sun. My tear ducts filled and overflowed as I read each entry, although my mind fought hard to keep the tears back. The evil, invective, and demonic spirits in Scotty stood out like a giant among children. *How did I not recognize this in him before marriage?*

As I studied the diary, I found paper strips between pages with written notes asking for more divine protection and the Blood of Jesus. My eyes widened, and scales seemed to fall from them. The mask of denial I'd worn during our courtship dropped from my face. The bitterness, evilness, demonic behaviors, obsessions, jealousies, and Scotty's association with satanic activity shone like a flashlight.

It's difficult to explain and may seem illogical, but I was so enveloped in Scotty's day-to-day mayhem that I couldn't meditate and reflect long enough to comprehend who I had yoked myself with. It was not until I emotionally detached from Scotty's despicable behavior that I could understand the magnitude of his abominations.

My journal showed that I prayed more and read and studied my Bible more during those traumatic courtship times. And after marriage, I stayed on my knees more than in my twenty years of Christian life.

One night, I was prompted to read the Book of Revelation. After reading the prophecies and the end-time predictions, I felt something stirring in my spirit. The word wormwood in the eighth chapter illuminated and stood higher. After reading the chapter three times, verse eleven jumped out at me.

> *"The name of the star is* **Wormwood***. A third of the
> waters turned bitter, and many people died from the
> waters that had become bitter"* Revelation 8:11 *(*NIV*)*.

Perceiving the Holy Spirit led me to the scripture because it related to our marriage; I whispered, "Jesus, Jesus, Jesus. Is the scripture saying that our marriage is bitter? Is it saying that many people will die spiritually from being associated with us and our marriage?" I didn't know what to think. *What does wormwood even mean?*

Grabbing my Webster's dictionary, I looked up the word to see how Mr. Webster described it. Wormwood (wurm wood): A bitter-tasting plant – a plant that yields a bitter extract; formerly, medicine for intestinal worms.

Cause of bitterness – something that causes somebody to feel bitter.

Medicine for intestinal worms? Yuk. My shoulders trembled, and my face tightened. Our marriage *was* mistrusting, non-communicative, chaotic, *bitter*, and dead. And Scotty's extreme wrath towards me increased after marriage. He poured all his anger, strife, mistrust, and hatred onto me. I was amazed that he hadn't somehow attempted to blame his daughter's death on me.

WORMWOOD.

Our marriage is a **Wormwood marriage***,* my mind said. Scotty had great bitterness towards me for some sin he imagined I committed. His continued chicanery and ingratitude caused me to harbor bitterness toward him. "This marriage will not survive if God doesn't change Scotty and me," I mumbled.

Many, many, many nights after he had fallen asleep and snored loudly, I sat on the side of the bed praying and sobbing, tears flowing like an opened dam down my face. I prayed for Scotty and for God to save our marriage. After failing in one union, I determined to make this marriage work, even if I had to play the roles of husband and wife.

The Holy Spirit didn't give up on me but comforted me, guided me, and helped me realize that I was not a failure.

Since I didn't recognize any spiritual growth after reading my diary, I viewed our marriage as a spiritually maturing experience.

After woefully admitting that marrying Scotty was not God's will, I still felt I had made my bed with fleas and now had to sleep in it.

God doesn't want robots serving him and gives us a free choice in our decision-making. There are consequences to every resolution we make, and if we decide out of the will of God, we may suffer consequences.

After months of marriage, I acknowledged that I was out of bounds for what Jehovah wanted. And until my life was back in spiritual order and in the right standing with God, I had decisions to make. I rationalized that if I prayed and fasted enough, studied the Bible more, and attended church faithfully, God would relent and bless me with a marvelously godly marriage.

Romans 8:28 (KJV) became my go-to scripture,

> *"And we know that all things work together for good to them that love God, to them who are the called according to His purpose."*

My mantra was that everything worked for my good because I loved God, not admitting I was out of Yahweh's plan and our marriage unsanctioned according to God's purpose.

My family, especially my mother and five sisters, Elana, Christy, Ashley, Tarrin, and Kameron, interceded for me daily. I was thankful I had the support of family and friends during those tumultuous times. None of my sisters or best friends were enthusiastic about my choice of mate, but they were willing to support me as long as I was happy.

Of course, I never told them about verbal abuse and jealousy before marriage.

After marriage, my sisters witnessed Scotty's controlling behaviors multiple times. They were polite but didn't have much to say to him. They had observed him embarrass me too many times. When they chose to converse with him, he perpetually slid something negative about me into the conversation.

My dad and five brothers, ages dispersed between us girls, tolerated Scotty better than the sisters. Their discussions included who played in the playoffs, all-star games, World Series, or Superbowl. Or what team traded, overpaid, and needed to exchange a jock.

DOUBLE STANDARDS

Deliberately working at being a virtuous, righteous, submissive, and obedient wife, I refused to argue with Scotty when he started a fight about some trivial issue. I prepared meals on time, kept the house spotless, and always made sure his clothes and linens were clean and ready for him. No matter how hard I tried, he was never satisfied and always found something to complain about.

One Saturday, as I folded his tee shirts and boxer shorts, his nose scrunched, and he said, "I'll wash my white clothes because they look dingy when you wash them."

I offered a clown's smile. "That sounds good. You can wash my white clothes too. Your white laundry looked whiter than mine anyway when I went to the laundry mat with you before we married."

He gave me one of those sideways, chin pointed to the floor, demonic looks, peering over his eyeglasses. I wasn't sure if his body language was saying, "No problem. Or it will be a cold day in purgatory before I wash your laundry." I'd have to wait and see if he washed my white clothes while doing his laundry.

Scotty liked buying expensive clothes, furniture, jewelry, and cars. His motto was, "You get what you pay for." He said if I purchased cheap and poorly made items, I should expect them to fall apart after the first wearing. He had bought expensive clothing and jewelry for me before our union. He stopped buying jewelry but continued to purchase my clothes. That way, he could control what I wore. He said, "The long skirts look more elegant than the shorter ones."

Therefore, my skirts were to my ankles, my blouses buttoned to the neck, and both were one size larger than my clothing size.

For some reason, he started spending more time with his female friends, buying expensive gifts for their birthdays, Valentine's Day, and Christmas, and even went on birthday cruises with two of them.

When I confronted him about gift buying, he said with a straight face, "Two of them have been my friends for years and helped me out of some financial situations. I'm not going to forget them just because I'm married."

My mouth gaped, and I crossed my arms. "You're the one who said I can't have male friends or associate with my ex-husband's family. You shouldn't be hanging with single women either."

Scotty's eyes rolled, and an exasperated sigh dropped.

"I feel sorry for the other women because they don't have a *man*."

My eyes widened, and my chin jutted. "You're not their man, and it is not your duty to buy them expensive gifts just because they aren't in a relationship." I sighed. "Then buy something less expensive."

If I had even murmured something about buying a male friend a gift or going on a cruise with another man, it would have been a drag-out, knock-down; you've got to be out of your mind fight. Well, I may be exaggerating a bit.

Scotty yawned and slumped into the recliner. I tapped a beat on the end table, studying Scotty and deciding to continue the discussion later.

At first, I didn't mind the gift giving too much because I'm generous and liked giving gifts for birthdays and special occasions. I initially thought it was considerate and kind of Scotty until it became excessive. It started with him mailing cards to three of his female friends, which was okay with me because getting a card when you didn't expect it could be uplifting and bring a smile to one's face.

In my opinion, it was beneficial to get a card when feeling unloved. But Scotty's card-giving progressed to sending flowers, which I intensely disliked. He rarely bought me flowers, saying, "It's not worth the money to buy roses because they die in two to three days anyway."

But I postulated that sending flowers would only be once or twice a year, and if it brought joy to his friends, it would be a blessing for us. By the end of the year, he was buying expensive oil paintings, vases, and crystals three to four times a year for several of his female friends. We managed separate financial accounts, and I had no control over his money.

The following night, I persisted with the previous night's conversation. "We need to talk, Scotty."

"Talk."

"I don't like you buying expensive gifts for your lady friends. It makes me feel disrespected and dishonored as your wife. You tell me that you love me and give me romantic greeting cards, but you don't demonstrate that you love me. Talking on the phone constantly with other women and buying them expensive gifts doesn't show love and respect for me. I want it to stop."

He interrupted before I finished my sentence. "I'm not spending one red cent of your money, and I can do what I want with my money."

"I'm trying to honestly tell you how I feel and get us to communicate. You always say that I nag and don't communicate. I'm trying to communicate with you as husband and wife."

"That sounds like nagging to me. You have a right to your feelings, and I have a right to mine, and I think I can do what I want with my hard-earned money." He grabbed his keys, shouting as he went out the door, "I'm going to pick up a birthday gift for my *sister.* I'll be back in a little while."

"He's incorrigible. I try to talk to him and tell him how I feel, and he makes a joke out of it," I roared, hoping he would hear me as the door slammed, knowing he was buying a gift for one of his friends.

Dr. Joyce had told me multiple times that communication was one of the keys to a good relationship. I was attempting to communicate. Neither of us were mind readers. Scotty had no idea what was happening in my head, nor did I know what was going on in his mind.

It took a risk for me to share my feelings, and Scotty thought it was a big joke.

Aunt Lucy had told me never to argue when I was angry, and I wasn't mad. She said to discuss the issues as soon as possible after they happened, and I didn't wait too long after the incidents to discuss them. Aunt Lucy said to pray before I discussed any concerns or conflicts with Scotty. She reassured me that the Holy Spirit would help me stay calm and give me peace, no matter how he responded. I did everything but pray. I had forgotten to pray before the discussion with Scotty.

Scotty was more sociable and kinder to strangers than his wife. He was still mean, hateful, and had a terrible attitude when dealing with me. *Why did he resent me so much?*

Our situation didn't improve after marriage, as I had imagined. I had felt confident that once we tied the knot, lived in the same house, and Scotty had me as his wife, things would improve in our relationship.

Around the fourth month of our union, the spirit of addiction raised its ugly head in Scotty. The ghosts of lying, manipulation, stealing, dishonesty, extreme anger, emotional adultery, and likely physical adultery followed addiction. Scotty misused his sleeping pills, tranquilizers, and pain pills as he did the codeine prescribed after his ankle surgery.

I said, "Scotty, your speech is slurred, and you stumble when you walk. You're taking too many pills at one time. You know the Ambien, Valium, and Tylenol number three are addictive, don't you."

He incoherently replied, "Don't worry about me and my meds. I get them from my doctor legally and won't get strung out."

I pinched the bridge of my nose and decided to try one last time. "Prescription drugs are the most addictive for the elderly. Just because your doctor writes a script doesn't mean you can't get hooked."

He mumbled words that seemed another language and limped to the bedroom. The following day, while eating dinner, he said, "I think I'm getting addicted to those pills, and I don't want nothing controlling me."

"I hear you," I replied. "I don't want anything controlling me either."

He stopped taking his sleeping pills and tranquilizers for six days and became jittery and irritable. The seventh night, he stumbled against the wall as he came to the kitchen, having resumed taking the meds. "My doctor will have to give me pills that don't make me jittery when I don't take them for a few days."

He saw his physician and returned with a different prescription for sleeping pills and tranquilizers. He claimed the pain pills didn't relieve his pain but continued to take them religiously. Scotty didn't drink alcohol or use illegal drugs but behaved like a street-using drug addict when he didn't take the pills. He couldn't eat or sleep, and irritability, nervousness, and quick temper seized him like a fly caught in a spider's web.

EMOTIONAL ADULTERY?

Scotty and I were not intimate as husband and wife, but I had not discovered any evidence that convinced me he was having an affair. He chatted on the phone with several female friends weekly and one daily, but I didn't sense he was having an experience with any of them, even though there were occasional low conversations. Most of their discussions concerned community events.

One time, when I narrowed my eyes and tightened my lips before giving him the telephone, Scotty said, "Nothing is going on with these women and me." He rubbed his chin. "I'm not one bit interested in any of them. They're board members seeking my input."

I forced a tight smile and handed him the phone.

Sometimes I even chatted with the caller before turning them over to Scotty. In the back of my mind, I didn't think a married man should be talking to other women as often as Scotty did, but I didn't want to appear jealous or mistrusting.

Everything would have turned back on me anyway, him saying I was just insecure.

I often considered saying something when he whispered in the back bedroom. But then, I thought my disapproval could be from my upbringing. My dad never had lengthy conversations with other women on the phone or in person. He always respected our mother and treated her as unique. Therefore, I concluded I was wrong for expecting my husband to treat me like my dad treated my mom. *Maybe his mom and dad had an open marriage where they had close friends of the opposite sex,* I thought.

It wasn't until I resumed attending my ladies' group that I seriously looked at Scotty's behavior with the other women. Shirley started a discussion on emotional adultery.

I had never heard of the term, probably because I hadn't been married for fifteen years, and the topic didn't interest me. As we discussed the behaviors of men committing emotional adultery, Scotty's behavior fit most of the signs.

My mind went to Scotty. He and I didn't communicate, but he talked about everything with his long-time female friend, Laverne. It seemed easier to discuss personal problems and Charlessa's death with her. He dropped everything if she called with a problem, and they had lunch or morning coffee weekly. I'm unsure if he talked about our marital problems with her, but I believe he vented to her about me when he was angry.

Shirley's stare brought my head back to the group. Like a dry sponge, I absorbed everything Shirley and the others said. My eyes lifted when Michelle said, "When a man accuses you of always cheating, he's probably cheating himself."

Shirley nodded, "Yep, you're right. But I'm not talking about cheating." She gazed at the group of women hanging on her words.

"I'm talking about when your man turns to another woman for emotional comfort and develops a deeper relationship with her than you, although they're just friends." She made quotation marks in the air, emphasizing the word friends.

Adelai jumped in, "Having your man share their deep secrets and emotions can be more dangerous than him having sex with her."

One of the ladies interrupted in a shrill tone, "You're right about that because then she has his mind."

Trying to participate in the discussion, I put my two cents worth in, but my mind was miles away, visualizing Scotty committing emotional adultery with Laverne.

A few other women added, "They don't work on their relationship with you." "He becomes more irritable with you." "He doesn't desire you anymore."

The statements flew over my head, but critical words crept through my ears and stayed. Scotty had been *irritable* with me for some time now, and after marriage, he didn't *desire* me or attempt to work on *improving* our relationship.

After the meeting, when I finally courageously confronted Scotty, he said, "Laverne has been my friend for over twenty years, and nothing is happening. I need someone to talk to. I can't talk to you because you're too argumentative and petty. Plus, she's a Christian woman and going to theology school." He sneered and dismissed me with a wave. "You need to get your mind out of the gutter and stop being so suspicious. Maybe I should watch who you're talking to since you are so concerned about my friend and me."

He limped away, came back, and stood nose to forehead with me, "And I am not going to stop talking to her! Don't bring it up again! Find yourself someone to talk to."

Out of the blue, he started volunteering with the youth ministry at our church. As a reward for perfect attendance, he took the young girls out to eat, to the theater, and to Christian concerts. When I observed him interacting with the teenage girls, a churning started in the pit of my stomach. I couldn't pinpoint why this uneasy, gnawing feeling possessed me. I never noticed any inappropriate touching, conversations, or behaviors between them. But my gut said something wasn't right. He seemed too chummy with the teenagers, not like a father figure but like a buddy. I volunteered to assist him, saying it didn't look appropriate for an older man to hang with young girls so often.

Of course, he accused me of having my mind in the gutter and making something out of nothing. After I told him I was volunteering, he snarled, "I was working with the youth department before I met you, and no one has said anything. I stopped for a while because I got too busy." His mouth twisted. "If the pastor thought it was inappropriate, he would have said something. I'm just trying to be a good Christian and a father figure to the young girls. Most don't have a daddy in the house, and many don't even know who their daddy is." He rubbed his eyes and glanced sideways.

"I don't want you working with me because you only want to work with the youth so you can spy on me."

As I stared at him with my arms folded in front of my stomach, emotional adultery scrolled through my head. I wondered if he was committing emotional adultery with the young girls. He preferred hanging with them more than with me and chatted like they were teen buddies.

I wondered if expensive gift-giving would be considered emotional adultery. Scotty never bought anything intimate that I was aware of, but the presents were costly, affecting the money he contributed to our household. Scotty even made a down payment on a car for Laverne but swore that nothing was going on between them.

He switched the conversation onto me, attempting to give me guilt for questioning him. "Hannah, your mind is always in the gutter. Just because you can't have a male friend without sleeping with him doesn't mean every woman is like you. Some women can be friends with men without sleeping with them."

An agonizing sigh crept from my mouth. I pressed my lips together, rolled my eyes, and strutted away with my chin lifted and shoulders high, steadfast that I would not cry because he had just suggested I was a slut and slept with all of my male friends.

To be honest, he didn't tell me about the down payment. When it took forever for our combined state income refund check to come, I started calls and research to discover the issue. I asked Scotty repeatedly if the check had come, and he replied, "No."

"Did you put it aside since both signatures are needed?" I asked. Scotty said, "No."

A week later, I asked, "Have you heard anything from the IRS, whether we owe money or our statements are being audited."

Each time Scotty responded that the check had not come, he was waiting for it too. By June, I figured the money must have gone to the wrong address, and someone had cashed and spent *our* money. I telephoned the state Internal Revenue Service department until I reached the correct department and verified our social security numbers, home address, phone number, and file date for the taxes.

My spirit stirred when the IRS representative asked, "Are you sure you didn't get the check? Did you talk to your husband?"

"My husband was waiting for the check and suggested I call the IRS to discover the hold-up."

The IRS representative rephrased my statement. "Your husband asked you to call us and said he had not seen the check? It shows in our records that the check was cashed in May."

Never in a thousand years did I think Scotty forged my name and cashed the check. I thought while I listened to papers shuffle on the other end. *Someone must have falsified our names and cashed the check. The postman had been leaving our mail at addresses two blocks away. He probably left our letter at the wrong address; someone else cashed it and spent the money.*

I exhaled. "What must I do to find out who cashed the check?"

"I can send you a copy of the endorsed check. If someone signed your name without your permission, it will become a legal matter, and you must contact the legal authority. The IRS does not handle those situations."

I thanked the representative for being patient and helpful. "How long will it take before I receive the copy?"

"You should receive the documents in two to three weeks."

I hung up the phone and thought about the situation, and a spirit of anger came upon me. I called my oldest sister and complained about the postal service leaving our refund check in the wrong mailbox, saying some dishonest person had cashed it with our names on it and had spent our money.

Two weeks later, my mouth gaped when the endorsed check came in the mail, and I dropped it onto the kitchen table. My eyes widened as I stared at the signatures and handwriting. I laid the check down, removed my glasses, picked the endorsed check up again, and held it closely, so I was positive it was Scotty's writing. It was Scotty's handwriting for both our names!

My right fist slammed the kitchen table, veins throbbing in my neck, and tears welling in my eyes. I didn't want to believe it, so I ransacked the house, looking for something else with Scotty's signature for comparison. I had to be sure it was his handwriting. I couldn't believe Scotty had forged my name, cashed the check, and spent sixty-five hundred dollars without telling me. Eventually, I found a charge card bill with his signature. It was Scotty's handwriting.

My head tilted, and my brows furrowed, dumbfounded. *Why would he do that? We were husband and wife. The check was assigned to Scotty and Hannah Brian, not Scotty or Hannah Brian. I had contributed overpaid taxes just like him. How could he look me in the eye each time I asked if our refund check had come and lied so genuinely? What did he do with the money? We were behind on our phone, gas, electric, insurance, credit cards, and mortgage because I stopped paying when Scotty refused to contribute. So I knew he had not used the money to pay past-due bills.*

I prayed and asked God to help me stay calm when I confronted Scotty about the false signature, anger still sizzling. "Lord, please do not let Scotty's attitude govern my behavior. Don't let me get angry and become nasty and unchristian because Scotty is cruel. Help me remember that I represent Jesus Christ, and I cannot act the way the world acts and respond the way the world responds."

When I discovered Scotty had signed my name and spent the money, I repented of the angry, accusatory spirit and the negative things I said about our postman and neighbors. I had bad-mouthed our innocent, efficient postman for two weeks, saying he was inefficient, lazy, and apparently couldn't read if he put people's mail in the wrong mailboxes.

Since Scotty spent his home time in the bedroom, it was a colossal task to urge him to eat at the dining room table. If not at his Medicare business, most of his time was secluded in the bedroom watching smutty reality shows depicting women as sluts and whores. The performances were where moms took their daughter's boyfriends, girls had babies by two brothers, sisters slept with brothers-in-law, and married women had affairs with other women.

He sat on the edge of the bed, hands clasped, yelling at the women on TV, "They should be strapped! I would have killed her! She deserves everything that happens to her! That's right, whip her butt!" It excited him to watch shows that made women appear immoral.

After much pleading, I encouraged him to eat dinner with me at the dining room table. Before he started dessert and finished the last bites of steak and potatoes on his plate, I thought the timing was right to ask him about the refund check. I folded my hands across my abdomen, inhaled deeply, and asked, "Did you forge my name and cash our refund check, Scotty?"

He looked up from his plate, chewed and swallowed the food in his mouth, and smiled one of his *I got over on you smiles*. He said, "Yep," rolled the last piece of Salisbury steak in gravy, put it in his mouth, and started reading the paper.

"Why did you falsify my name when I was here to sign the check? And why didn't you tell me the check had come and you had cashed it instead of having me think that someone else had cashed and spent our money?" A long, exasperated sigh fell. "I must have asked you about that check twenty times, and you looked me dead in the eye and said you had not seen it and that it had not come."

He continued reading the paper, pursed his lips, and ignored me as though I was talking to the refrigerator or stove.

My voice rose, and my fists clenched. "I'm talking to you, Scotty. You can at least acknowledge me. I want to know what happened with the money."

"I had stuff to do with the money. You've been acting funny lately."

My head shook as my face warmed. "But you forged my name. That's illegal!" I paused for effect. "That check belonged to both of us! It said Scotty and Hannah Brian, not Scotty or Hannah Brian. You had no right to sign my name without my knowledge and cash the check without telling me!"

He clasped his hands behind his head. "Sue me! I told you I had stuff to do with the money. So get off my back before you make me angry!"

After one last attempt at finding out what he did with the money and noticing his body tighten and fists clenched, I left the table and went to the living room. For several weeks, I played a private investigator. I snooped around in his secret drawers until I found the contract to the car dealership with Scotty as co-signer for Lavern's vehicle.

Not wanting to start a fight by telling him I searched his personal belongings, I got verification from the dealership when I showed them the contract.

With verification, I challenged Scotty, "I test-drove a new Honda Civic today." Saliva from nervousness pooled in my mouth, and I swallowed hard. "When I said I would be back with my husband, Scotty Brian, the salesman said he sold a new Honda to you a few months back." I lifted my head and sat taller in my chair, locking eyes with him.

His face reddened, and he looked at his lap. After a few beats, he said, "Laverne came to me crying, said her husband had left her, took the car, and she needed a vehicle to get to work, or she would lose her job and not be able to take care of her children," his voice high-pitched and rapid. He exhaled, and his tone slowed. "Laverne didn't have anyone else to help her. I told you, Laverne, and I was friends before I met you, and I've known her longer than I've known you."

His shoulders squared, and he pushed his chest out. "She would do the same for me."

While I stared, pouting with my arms across my chest, he brazenly said, "You would do the same for your sisters or girlfriends if they needed help!"

"I would have told you and wouldn't have forged your name on a check."

He stood to leave. "It's over with now. I can't take the car back."

I followed. "It hurt me that you took all the money that belonged to *both* of us. You could have told me you were helping Lavern." He stopped, and I bumped into him. "Sorry."

"Stop nagging me. You just like to fuss."

"We're having difficulty keeping up with our household expenses, so I thought we'd use the money to catch up on our bills."

His eyes narrowed, and his lips pressed together. "That little check wouldn't make that big of a difference. My business will pick up, and when it does, I'll pay all the bills, okay? Now stop following me." He limped into the bedroom and closed the door.

I stood before the door, deciding if I wanted to press my luck while he responded or wait until another time to finish our discussion. Everything I didn't want him doing for his female friends swam through my head. *I didn't like him buying expensive gifts for women and didn't want him making a down payment on a car. Signing my name was a federal offense, even if we were married, and I could sue him if I chose to do so.*

My mind said it was futile to continue the discussion because when he started purchasing the expensive items, I told him I didn't like him buying gifts for other women. As if I was telling a teen to clean their room, Scotty had mumbled, "Uh huh," and sent mums to one of his lady friends the next day. I neglected to pray about the situation or seek guidance from the Holy Spirit as I should have.

THE CHICAGO FIASCO

<hr>

For weeks after returning from our New York outing, Scotty acted like he was walking and sitting on pins and needles, anxious to go to Chicago and find Boston Matheson.

We got up early one Saturday morning and drove to Chicago's Lake Shore Drive, the location of BM's business. Scotty pulled over to the side of the road, took his wallet out, and pulled out BM's trucking business card. He read the name and address of his trucking company out loud. "His business is about another hour south of here."

Scotty tucked the card back into his wallet, merged with traffic, and headed to the address on the card. As we pulled up in front of the building, we spotted Boston and three young men entering a white Cadillac Escalade. BM and the muscular fellow with him on the train hopped in the back. Scotty waited until they pulled into traffic, and two cars were behind them before he swerved behind the second car.

He followed two cars behind the Escalade and was fortunate that when one of them turned, another car sped in its place, making Scotty confident the Escalade hadn't spotted the tail. BM made stops on

Chicago's east, north, west, and south sides as far as Hammond, Indiana.

After hours of following BM, I said, "He must have friends all over Chicago." I looked at the gas hand. "We're going to need gas soon. We don't want to run out of gas in a strange neighborhood."

Scotty glanced at the fuel monitor. "We're good. We still got a fourth of tank left."

"Why don't you pull alongside his car at the next stop he makes and let him know we're in Chicago and wanted to say hello."

He didn't answer. For some reason, he was intent on tracking BM, which made me nervous as we entered dangerous neighborhoods.

The escalade made a U-turn at one of the intersections and headed back toward Chicago's downtown loop. Boston's side window rolled down, and he looked directly at us. My heart rate sped up. "I think he suspects we're following him, Scotty. Why don't you catch them and remind him of who we are?"

"Shut up! I know what I'm doing."

"I'm sure he doesn't remember us." I balled a fist under my chin. "I'd be concerned too if I spotted a car following me for hours."

Scotty pulled to the curb, watching the Escalade in his sideview mirror. When they stopped for a red light a block up the street, Scotty quickly swerved into the left lane and made a quick U-turn heading south. He continued tailing BM, trying to stay two to three cars behind but not too far back that he couldn't spot the white Escalade. We had trailed them all day, and it was now dark outside. Scotty had followed them to the Hammond/Chicago border when the Escalade quickly pulled to the right and parked.

Scotty cruised past the parked car. "Look straight ahead! Don't look at them!"

"Why are we following them, Scotty? What do you expect to find out by following him? I don't like this, and my stomach is twirling like I might throw up." I inhaled several times deeply and massaged my belly to lessen the nausea.

Scotty kept looking in his rearview mirror for the car to move, but it stayed parked on the street. "That doesn't make sense. They've made stops at office buildings, bars, and restaurants; why are they parked on the street here in Indiana?"

"Maybe they're meeting someone at that spot, or maybe someone lives in one of the homes they're parked in front of."

Scotty's lips jerked to the side. "But no one has gotten out of the car, and no one has come to the Caddie. I would have seen them get out." Scotty's brows knit together above his nose. "I've been driving 25 miles per hour, stopped at two red lights, and no one has moved from the car. I'm going back around."

"Don't do that, Scotty!" my voice was more high-pitched than I wanted. "Please don't go back. Let's go home."

He made a right turn at the third stoplight, another right turn, and a third right at the next stop sign, expecting to loop around to where the Cadillac was parked. Instead, we ended up on a dead-end street. As he shifted into reverse, bright headlights beamed into our car from the vehicle blocking us. My heart started palpitating. *Who is that? Have some robbers or murderers cornered us on this dead-end street?*

Scotty shifted the gears into park and waited for the footsteps to reach our vehicle strolling from the bright lights shining behind us. "Hand me that pistol from the glove compartment."

As I opened the compartment, someone tapped on Scotty's window. Scotty lowered the glass, and a young man wearing a three-piece suit and sunglasses with a brutal, thug-like persona glared at Scotty, his lips pressed together.

He looked inside our vehicle, eyed me, and then focused on Scotty. "You've been following us all day, and Boss Man wants to know what's up?"

Scotty pressed his back against the seat's cushion.

"Who's Boss Man?"

The young man bit his bottom lip. "The man you've been tailing all day, old man. Don't play games with me 'cause I ain't the one."

BM had changed cars at some point and had us cornered on a dead-end street.

Scotty pulled the business card from his wallet and gave it to the young man. "We met Boston on the train to New York. He said we could look him up whenever we were in Chicago."

The young man took the card, peered at it over his sunglasses, and stared at Scotty intently. "That still don't tell me why you've been following us all day."

"Would you take the card to BM and tell him it's Scotty and Hannah from the train? We hoped he would stay at one spot long enough for us to come in and chat with him."

The young man shook his head and frowned. His body language said, "I don't believe you." He peered over his sunglasses at Scotty again and leaned his head inside to snag a better look at me before strolling back to a Silver Mercedes Benz.

For ten minutes while we waited for BM or the young man to return, I twisted my wedding ring, played with my hair, and dried my clammy hands with napkins from the glove compartment. Finally, the young man swaggered back to our car, gave Scotty a piece of paper with an address, and told us to meet them in an hour.

Forty-five minutes later, Scotty parked in front of an expensive restaurant downtown and watched for Boston Matheson to arrive.

Fifteen minutes later, I said, "It's 7:00. We'd better go inside so he doesn't think we stood him up."

"I'm waiting for him to go in first."

I exhaled loudly. "Boston could already be inside. He switched cars on us once already."

Scotty gave me a sideways glance, opened his door, and slid out of the vehicle.

When we stepped inside, we weren't sure whether to say we had a meeting with Boston Matheson or to sit and wait for him. BM and his entourage strolled in as the Maitre d' looked up from the reservation list. He stepped to Scotty, eyeballed him, and then shook his hand.

Scotty said, "We were in Chi-town and –"

The corners of BM's lips upturned, and his eyes crinkled at the corners. He interrupted Scotty. "Yeah, yeah, the old man from the train." His head nodded. "I remember you from the train and how charming and pleasant you were." He flashed a smile. "And kind of nosey, if I remember. What's up, old man?" He moved closer to Scotty's right ear. "I'm sure you have an excellent explanation for why you've been dogging me all day."

Is this the same man we met on the train, talking street slang instead of the perfect English he had spoken on the train? I glanced up at BM, and he gave me his award-winning smile. That beautiful smile, with those gleaming, straight, white teeth, was undeniable. It was the same handsome man, but he seemed different tonight.

Scotty continued, "You invited us to look you up the next time we were in Chicago." Scotty posted a clown's smile, joked, and reminisced about the train trip. "Well, I'm in Chicago, and I looked you up. You gave us your business card with your trucking company's address. We went there, and you got in a car before we could get to you. I decided to follow you until you got to your next stop." He lifted his cane. "You know that I move slowly, and before I could slide out of the car to flag you down, you were on the move again." Scotty grinned. "That was some train trip. The food was good for rail food, and that game went into overtime, remember?"

Until BM finished his conversation with Scotty, the Maitre d' waited patiently, then politely said, "Would you like to be seated now, Mr. Matheson? And how many are in your party?"

While seated at our table, Scotty continued reminding BM about the train trip and how nice he was to us. Boston dropped his questions about Scotty following him. I figured he thought Scotty was a forgetful older adult.

The three men with BM were respectful but not friendly. They sat at a table facing the door while we enjoyed an incredible five-course meal and conversation with Boston. He seemed like a nice man while we sat and interacted with him. But I was wise enough to understand he didn't have three brutal bodyguards because he was a wealthy entrepreneur.

After dinner, BM and Scotty enjoyed a cigar and laughed as Scotty told jokes. Scotty invited Boston to Madison since he said he had never been. "We can check out a Badgers game when you come."

"Maybe I'll do that one day soon. But, Mr. Scotty, call first the next time you want to visit me."

BM escorted us to our car and asked if we needed directions, and Scotty said, "No."

Boston kissed me on the cheek. "It was a pleasure seeing you again, Mrs. Scotty." He flashed a smile.

"You can call me Hannah." I returned the smile.

"Hannah, it is." He tapped his shoulder to Scotty's shoulder while shaking his hand. "Have a safe trip back to Madison."

We waved goodbye as we drove away. I held my breath, waiting for Scotty to yell about Boston kissing me on the cheek. He didn't appear to have noticed the kiss. Scotty mumbled, more to himself than me. "It will be too difficult to catch BM alone in Chicago. I'll have a better chance of getting him alone in Madison. I've got to convince him to visit us."

I added my two cents, although Scotty didn't ask for my input. "He's going to have his bodyguards wherever he goes," I insisted. "I don't think you can get him alone in Madison either. Why don't you forget about this foolishness? Let it go, Scotty, please."

"You don't know squat, Hannah. I keep telling you that! Remember that I am the master of game-playing! I ran the streets when I was younger, and it's no different now than it was then, just more toys and technology for them to play with."

"But Scotty, you...."

"I will not let it go, and that's it! So, forget it, and don't bring that up to me again. Do you understand me?"

"Yes, I understand you clearly. I will not discuss it again. But I still think it's foolish and dangerous, especially since you've told me rumors about how notorious and heartless Boston is."

"What did I say? Didn't I say I don't want to discuss it again?"

My shoulders shrugged. "Okay."

Scotty pulled in at the first gas station he spotted, filled the tank, and got directions to Madison.

So Scotty went to work coaxing BM to Madison for a weekend. He invited him to bar-be-cues, baseball games, basketball games, and holiday parties, but Boston never came. Scotty tried to present himself as a loving, concerned surrogate father, remembering BM was adopted. As Scotty lured Boston into his satanic trap, BM's attitude changed slowly toward Scotty. With our landline on speaker, when he chatted on the phone with Scotty, his voice sounded less tense and more relaxed. Sometimes they talked for an hour. He began viewing Scotty as a surrogate dad and father figure.

Both of us were surprised when Scotty received a call from Boston saying he would be in Madison the next day and would call Scotty once he got in the city. I should say that I was surprised.

Scotty said, "I knew I would eventually attract BM to Madison. It was just a matter of time and being persistent."

He tilted his head in my direction. "You give up to easy, Hannah. You have to stay at it. You have to be tenacious. You must know what you want and stick with it until you get it!"

After lecturing me on capturing what I wanted, he remembered Boston would be in town tomorrow.

"That doesn't give me much time to plan an ambush or tactical strategy to kill him," he said, limping to the bedroom and closing the door.

While he made several calls to various people, I eavesdropped, hoping to discover his plan so I could figure out a way to warn Boston Matheson. My mouth gaped when I heard Scotty discussing drug territories with a Madison drug lord. "Boston Matheson, you might know him as BM, is trying to take over the south Madison territory, man... I'm just trying to give you a tip... How do I know?... I know Boston Matheson personally. I've often been to his Chicago house, nightclub, and dinner with him... Why am I telling you if we're such great friends? It's something personal between me and BM, and I don't care to discuss it with you. You can take the tip or not."

Scotty sighed into the receiver. "I don't care what you do, just giving you a heads up that BM will be in Madison tomorrow, and I'm sure it's to check out the south side territory. If you want to keep it, you may want to be in the area tomorrow."

Scotty hoped to start a drug war between BM and the dealers in Madison, hoping the kingpins would do his dirty work for him. He would execute revenge on Boston Matheson and still keep his hands clean. Plus, he figured it would be easier for the dealers and thugs to get to BM than himself.

The next day, Scotty was as anxious as a cat on a hot tin roof. He picked up the landline to ensure it was working, peered through the blinds every quarter hour, and went to the door every time a car pulled in front of our house.

When he didn't hear from BM as expected, Scotty was furious, slamming books to the floor and pounding his cane against the wall. "That chump ain't gonna play me," Scotty said after he calmed down. "I'm the *Master of Game* playing. I was running game before that chump was born." He watched the clock tick away, tick tock, tick tock, tick tock, and when the hands reached 5:00 p.m., he picked up the phone and called BM's direct line.

"Interstate Trucking, this is BM. How can I make your day better?"

"BM, this is Scotty. I've been waiting for you all day. Hannah cooked a special meal just for you, and you didn't show or call to tell us you weren't coming." He attempted to hide the anger in his voice.

"I'm sorry, Mr. Scotty. I really am. Give my apologies to Miss Hannah. I ran into some problems with some deliveries down south. I'm in a little town in Arkansas called Helena. Have you heard of it?"

"Helena? Yeah, I've met several people from Helena. Well, call me when you're back in Chicago, and we can set something else up. Okay?"

"Sure. I'm getting into the busy time of year for my business, so it may not be until sometime next year. But I will come to Madison very soon. I'm curious to tour the city and find out what it offers besides a university."

Scotty scowled and rolled his eyes. "You take care, man. I'll probably give you a call tomorrow."

"Yes, sir. Peace."

CHAOS CONTROL CONFRONTATION

L enny spent six months in county jail for disorderly conduct related to the incident at our wedding. After much begging by me and persuasion by Markus, Shirley's husband, Scotty dropped all charges of attempted homicide or threat with a deadly weapon. Lenny's pistol was registered.

By the end of our first year of marriage, I was out of the loop regarding the events that Shirley and Michelle hosted due to my fear that Scotty would embarrass me. Therefore, I wasn't attending the multiple celebrations as before marriage. I had not spoken with Adelai or Lenny since the wedding.

Headed home from dinner at Cracker Barrel, the golden setting sun in the west looked like it was floating atop the water. I pointed. "Look at the sun, Scotty. Isn't it gorgeous?"

Scotty's neck twisted in the direction of the diminishing sun. "Yeah, it's pretty."

Scotty stayed on the street rather than taking the highway home as he usually did. My eyes widened as my head turned left and right. "You missed our entrance to the expressway. Where are we going?"

Scotty glanced over his shoulder toward the highway.

"Did I ever show you where I grew up as a child?"

"No. Is that where we're going?"

"I haven't been in my old neighborhood in years." A smile crossed his face. "I wonder if the diamond is still there where I played baseball."

The orange-red ball of light in the sky disappeared, and shadows of darkness crept around us. As we drew nearer to the park, streetlights popped on. I sat with my hands crossed in my lap, surveying the neighborhood. "You grew up on the east side of town?"

He nodded. "There were only three Black families when my family moved here." He glanced at some of the homes and people surrounding the park. "Look at it now. All I see are Black folks."

"The area still looks nice. It shows that the property owners value and care for their neighborhood."

Scotty drove a loop around the playground, pointing to areas where he practiced for the track team and played basketball. He then headed to the baseball diamond. After stopping in the middle of the street to watch a few pitches and a couple of batters hit the ball, Scotty pulled off and drove toward the main road, heading out of the park.

Of all the people in the world for us to see crossing the street, Lenny strode several feet ahead with a bat and baseball mitt. When I looked at Scotty, his jaws clenched, and his lips arched to the side. He grunted, pressed the accelerator, and sped in Lenny's direction.

Instinctively, my hands grabbed the steering wheel as I shouted, "Don't do it, Scotty!" The vehicle swerved to the right.

Lenny's head lifted, hearing the screech of the brakes, and he spotted a car accelerating, heading in his direction. He jumped out of the way onto the curb but lost his balance, falling to the grassy ground. Scotty jerked the car into reverse, mashed the accelerator, and tried to back over Lenny while he was down.

Lenny jumped up, stood in batting position, and smashed the rear windshield on the driver's side as we backed up. Scotty jammed on the brakes and threw the gear into park. Lenny sprinted to the front and smashed the driver's side of the front window.

Scotty pushed to open the door to step out, but it didn't budge.

Breathing rapidly, I held Scotty's arm in a vise grip. "Let's go home, Scotty. This behavior doesn't make sense. One of you is going to get hurt or end up dead."

"I'm not scared of that negro." He glared at Lenny through the fractured glass.

Lenny stood near Scotty's door with the bat held at a forty-five-degree angle, ready to strike Scotty in the head if he stepped out.

"Give me my piece!" Scotty demanded. "Look in the glove compartment!"

I hesitated, hoping it would allow Lenny to trot to his car and drive away. But he stood like a statue, in batting position, waiting for Scotty to open the door. I didn't move, so Scotty reached over me and searched the glove compartment for his twenty-two-caliber pistol until it was in his hand. He pulled it out and checked to ensure a cartridge was inside and the safety was off. *Is Lenny foolish or what? Doesn't he see what Scotty is doing in this car? Does Lenny think a bat can beat a bullet? Maybe he thinks he can hit Scotty before he has an opportunity to pull the trigger. Why doesn't he leave? Phew, men and their egos.*

I started praying, as always, when I didn't know what to do. Scotty thought for a moment, put his left hand on the door handle, and gently began to open it.

Do something, Hannah. You can't let him open that door. "Scotty."

He turned and looked at me with his cold, mean, hateful eyes. "What!" he yelled.

"Think about what you're doing. Lenny is not worth you going back to prison. What about all the work you've done with the youth ministry? It will all be lost because no one else will be as dedicated as you are."

He stared at me as if a baboon had talked to him. "I told you I don't mind going back to prison. This guy has insulted me too many times. It will be worth returning to the penitentiary to see him lying dead, flat on his back." He lifted on the door handle, and the door cracked open slightly.

Lenny stood like a carving, knees bent, bat over his shoulder, staring into the vehicle.

"What should I do, Jesus?" I mumbled. My head lifted, and I spotted a police car. I exhaled. "Don't open the door, Scotty. There's a police car driving in this direction."

Our vehicle obstructed traffic in the middle of the street due to cars parked on both sides. Scotty snapped the door shut and drove to the stop light, allowing the police officers to move past.

"Thank you, Jesus," I whispered. I looked in my sideview mirror, and Lenny pointed in our direction as he talked to the police officers.

Seeing the law enforcement officers stare at us and rush to their car, Scotty swerved at the stop light and headed north to the low-income apartment buildings. He paralleled parked between two automobiles facing the street and turned off his lights and ignition. The police offi-cers drove slowly past the apartment building to the end of the block and made a U-turn. They headed back toward the parking structure and turned left into the parking lot just as a truck sped past them, driving fifty or sixty miles per hour in a thirty-mile-per-hour speed zone. The officers reversed, put their sirens on, and rushed after the speeding motorist.

"Wow!" A deep exhale escaped. "That was a close call," I exclaimed.

Scotty said nothing. He turned on the ignition and headlights and drove out of the parking structure, away from the apartment building. Returning to the street where we had seen Lenny, Scotty studied each side, peeping into vehicles hoping to spot Lenny again. When he didn't see him, he turned right at the end of the block and headed toward home.

Each time my family invited me to a social gathering, Scotty said his back, knees, or hips hurt or his blood sugar was low. He aimed to isolate me from my family, as he had done with my friends. But my older sister would not allow it. When I didn't attend the fiftieth birthday celebration for my brother, Willie, my five sisters came to our house after the festival to ensure I was okay.

When the doorbell rang, it was 10 p.m. As usual, Scotty was back in the bedroom, and I was in the living room watching a Trinity Broadcasting Network special. Since neither of us was expecting guests, we ignored the booming buzzer.

After a few moments, pecking on my dining room, kitchen, and living room windows caught my attention. I stood to see who had the gall to tap on our window at 10 p.m. and heard my name repeated.

A recognizable voice came from the living room window. "Hannah, are you in there?"

Another familiar voice came from the kitchen area. "Are you okay, Hannah?"

Then, a recognizable, braying voice came from the dining room area. "Hannah, you're not asleep. Open the door!"

It sounds like my sisters' voices, but why are they here this late? They could have phoned me. Then I remembered that the ringer volume was set low on my landline phone, and my mobile died and was charging.

As I rushed to open the front door, praying mom and dad were well and no one was hurt or dead, my cell phone rang. I snatched it from the charger as I headed to the front door. "Hello..."

My older sister, Elana, said in a high-pitched tone, "What's going on in there, Hannah? Why aren't you opening the door? Are you being held hostage? Has he hurt you?" She disliked Scotty more than any of my sisters.

I ended the call and shouted as I raced to the front door. "I'm headed to open the door now. When I opened it, I said, "I didn't know it was you guys. I'm fine, not a hostage, and he didn't hurt me." My five sisters marched in like military soldiers going to battle, nonsmiling with a no non-sense, serious expression on their faces. They hugged and kissed me, then walked through my house, investigating and inspecting every room like CSI investigators at a crime scene.

Elana stopped in front of the closed bedroom door, pointed at it, shrugged her shoulders, and shook her head up and down. I quickly shook my head from side to side, beckoning for her to return to the living room. When I sat on the sofa, they sat quietly around me. Ten eyes stared, waiting for me to tell them what was happening and why I wasn't at the celebration.

When I said nothing, Elana glanced at our sisters and then at me with one raised eyebrow. "Why weren't you at Willie's fiftieth birthday party? You can only have a fiftieth birthday party one time."

Before I could respond, Christy interjected. "What took you so long to open the door?"

Tarrin asked in a soft voice. "Are you sure that you're okay?"

"You don't look right. Is everything really okay?" Kameron rose and stood over me, looking intently into my eyes.

"We're worried about you, Hannah. You haven't been your normal self lately and never miss a family event." Ashley said with concern.

I didn't want to discuss my marital problems then and didn't think sitting in my living room with Scotty only twenty feet away was the proper location either. I forced a smile, kissed Kameron's forehead, and pretended everything was fine. "Scotty wasn't feeling well, so I stayed home with him. He got sick as we were walking to the door. I wasn't expecting any company this late, so I didn't answer the door."

Elana interrupted. "Is he dying?"

"Is who dying?" My brows furrowed, and my shoulders shrugged as I looked at my other sisters.

Elana pressed her lips together, rolled her eyes, and said, "Your husband. If he wasn't dying, we don't see why you couldn't have at least made an appearance at the party."

My brows creased, and confusion caused my head to dip. I covered my eyes with my hand when it sank in what Elana was implying.

Tarrin added. "Everyone wanted to know why you weren't there, and everyone was worried about you, especially mother."

Kameron said in a honeyed voice, "It's because you never miss family events, Hannah. And everyone was worried."

A tired sigh dropped from my lips, and my shoulders slumped. "I'll call Mother tomorrow and tell her I'm okay and apologize for not attending the birthday celebration. I am sorry."

Elana interrupted again. "For future events, one of us will pick you up. You can't stop being with family like you've stopped socializing with friends. It's not healthy for you, Hannah."

I sat without interrupting and listened as they described the beautiful birthday party I missed.

Elana said as they left my house, "The only way you can miss a family event is that Scotty will be on his deathbed."

After my sisters' intervention, I didn't miss any more family festivities. Scotty realized that my sisters would not allow him to isolate me from family and that they were serious about me not missing another family celebration.

Scotty still pretended to have pain or some sickness on the day of a family gala. He would not go with me and called me selfish and uncaring because I left him home alone sick. He would laugh and talk on the phone or watch television with no complaints until an hour before the party. And then, out of nowhere, fake pains materialized. I finally realized he used the faked illness to try to isolate me from my family.

Elana saw through Scotty's phoniness the first time she met him, and Scotty knew that she did not particularly care for him. I think the demonic spirits in him were afraid of the righteousness in Elana. The impish spirits didn't raise their ugly heads when she was around. She lived the Christian life she talked about and was not intimidated by the evil spirits in Scotty. Therefore, he said nothing when she picked me up.

HE'S NOT YOUR DADDY

---

*B*itterness. *Grievous. Resentment. Revengefulness. Death.*

While Scotty was away celebrating a birthday with one of his female friends, I reflected on the revelation from the Holy Spirit comparing our marriage to the star **Wormwood.** ".......

A great star shot from the sky, flaming like a torch, and fell on a third of the rivers and springs; the name of the star was Wormwood. A third of the water turned to wormwood, and great numbers of people died from drinking the water because it had been made bitter" Revelations 8: 10-11 (REB).

I sensed I was in spiritual disobedience and out of position for God's plan for my life, but I couldn't pull it together.

Or I refused to pull it together.

Being Queen Pollyanna, I was the ultimate optimist, thinking that one day I would wake up and things would be better in our marriage. Scotty would be my perfect husband, and the epiphany of our marriage being Wormwood would be unfulfilled.

Jehovah had a plan and purpose for my life, but He needed my undivided attention first. As I went through the trials and tribulations with Scotty, Yahweh eventually got my attention.

God uses what and whom He wishes to accomplish His purposes. God Jehovah even used a donkey to execute His goal.

> *"The Lord then made the donkey speak, and she said to Balaam, 'what have I done? This is the third time you have beaten me.' Balaam answered, 'you have been making a fool of me. If I had had a sword with me, I should have killed you on the spot.' But the donkey answered, 'am I not still the donkey which you have ridden all your life? Have I ever taken such a liberty with you before?' He said, 'no.' Then the Lord opened Balaam's eyes: he saw the angel of the Lord standing in the road with his sword drawn, and he bowed down and prostrated himself"* Numbers 22: 28-31 (REB).

My mother told Scotty at our wedding that her daughter was getting a husband and not a *daddy*. Her wisdom had picked up Scotty treating me like his child, servant, or maid. When my mom made the toast, I smiled, thinking he knew *I was his wife and not his child. Daddies don't sleep with their daughters.* I expected us to sleep together as husband and wife after marriage.

That never happened. Scotty did not cuddle or attempt to have sex after we said, "I do." Possibly, he could have viewed me as his child since he was not conjugating with me.

On one visit before marriage, my mom made an odd statement. "Men promise to give you the stars when they're courting you and give you the *sun* after they've married you."

"What does that mean, Mom? They give you the sun after they've married you," I asked, intrigued by the statement.

"It means, my dear daughter, that some men will say anything to bait you to marry them. They promise you the stars on a platter and the world as your oyster. But after they've married you, the relationship becomes *hot, hot, hot,* like the sun's rays, with jealousy, anger, confusion, and frustration." Her head shook. "The sun is hot and uncomfortable, right? Well, these types of men give you more chaos than peace, confusion than comfort, anger than joy, jealousy than trust, and frustrations than contentment."

"You have so much wisdom, Mom," I said. I didn't share that she described Scotty to the T, not knowing she had already detected Scotty's jealousy when she studied him and me together.

After months of marriage, I began to understand what she meant. I loved and respected my mother but didn't always heed her advice. When she said relationships get hot after marriage, I thought, *"All men are not like that. There are still a few good and decent men left. I can handle Scotty. He's a bit jealous, but I don't think he'll become worse after we're married.*

A stubborn, stiff-necked, and obstinate streak struck me sometimes, and I thought I was in control. I don't say that with pride but with the utmost humility. I thought I was controlling my life, but demonic spirits were behind the scenes orchestrating every detail.

My mother was not the type to dictate her children's lives, telling us who to marry, where to live, and where to work. She allowed us to make our own mistakes and prayerfully learn from the blunders we made. It wasn't until I began to experience the *hot, hot, and hotter* in my marriage that I understood what my mom was trying to tell me. The verbal abuse, condemnations, and accusations felt like a flaming torch and burned my soul. I understood why the Holy Spirit had shown me that our marriage was a *Wormwood marriage*.

Sadly, we don't often appreciate the wisdom of our elders until it's too late. I hopped from the scorching flames into the fiery furnace when I married Scotty.

Scotty accused me of having an affair with every Tom, Dick, Harry, and John. Every night of our marriage, we argued about some strange man that Scotty accused me of having an experience with.

I volunteered with the prison ministry at our church, and our prison team visited one of the state prisons monthly. The inmates knew us only as Brother Williams, Brother Jones, Sister Winston, or Sister Brian. The prisoners had no personal information on the team. Our purpose was to witness, be a light in the darkness, and prayerfully lead some to the saving knowledge of Jesus Christ.

Well, Scotty accused me of having affairs with the prison inmates. I had no idea he felt I would stoop that low to be with a man. I couldn't understand why he thought so little of my morals now than before our wedding. He said I was his God-sent soul mate before matrimony.

One evening, when I strolled into the house, Scotty followed me to our bedroom. "Did you give our private home number to one of the inmates?"

My mouth gaped, and I stared at him with wide eyes, not responding.

He stood so close that when I turned, I bumped into him. "We've been getting collect phone calls from the state prison, and the caller asks specifically for Hannah Brian."

My lips pressed together and twisted to the side. An exasperated sigh dropped while I rubbed my forehead.

"Why didn't you just say no to the collect call?" My hands went to my hips, and my chin jutted toward him.

His head tilted. "Because they asked for you by name, and I thought it might have been a family member."

"I don't have any family in prison."

"Then why did he ask for you by name?"

My shoulders shrugged. "I don't know, Scotty. We tell the inmates our last names; my name is in the phone book. Maybe he had nothing else to do. He searched the phone book, found my name, and called to ask me to send him money." My hands opened in front of me, and my shoulders shrugged again.

"Why you?"

A loud exhale sounded. "The convict probably called all of the prison team."

Scotty quieted as he stared at the phone. "Well, I don't want him calling again."

"Just hang up if anyone from the prison calls again."

In my heart, I don't believe anyone telephoned from the prison. It was another of Scotty's games to frazzle me and study my reaction. Strangely, no one called in the evening when I was home, but they always called during the day when Scotty was alone. I never received one call from an inmate in the evening or when I happened to be off during the day.

If inmates were shrewd enough to find my home phone number, they would also have been smart enough to locate my work numbers at the hospital and my business. I never received a collect call at any of my jobs.

Scotty's evil imagination and depraved thinking made him believe prisoners called our home. Possibly, the evil spirits in Scotty gave him messages of the phone ringing, and in his head, the voice of some male from prison asked for me. I had no idea what was going on in Scotty's head. But the thoughts caused fights about men supposedly calling me from jail.

I recalled the one time he admitted that he struggled with mental health issues when I broke up with him. But I wasn't sure if it was manipulation to woo me back or the truth. His behaviors were so bizarre that mental health could have caused many of them, but I believe his association with a psychic and the occult contributed to most of it.

Scotty allowed the demonic spirits to destroy him and our marriage. He argued with such passion that I honestly think that he believed the calls were valid. I tell you the truth, not one day passed that Scotty didn't find something to be vociferous about. It was 365 days a year of deviousness and denunciatory behavior.

HUMILITY AND HUMILIATION

Months after the park incident, I bumped into Lenny at the Marriott Hotel. Both of us were attending a business conference. Recessing for lunch, I crashed into Lenny in the lobby.

At first, the conversation was awkward as we fumbled with small talk, avoiding eye contact. After talking about our conferences and Adelai, I finally said, "I'm sorry for all that has happened, Lenny. I don't know what else to say." Both of my shoulders rose. "Scotty is super jealous and sometimes lets his possessiveness get the best of him."

"Don't worry about it, Hannah." He looked toward the marbled black and brown floor. "I'm sorry for disrupting your wedding. I had an anger issue that I hadn't dealt with." He finally made eye contact. "Adelai stuck with me, and we're doing fine. We've talked about relocating and getting out of Wisconsin. I want to go to a warmer climate, but Adelai doesn't want to move too far away from her family."

My eyes on his, I said, "I miss you and Adelai, and I'm truly sorry that we aren't friends like we used to be. Shirley told me that you two finally got married. Congratulations!"

"Thanks. Yea, we jumped the broom and did it." He stepped closer. "I know it's not my business, Hannah, but what do you see in him? I would never have imagined you being married to that guy. He must compensate somewhere for all of the crazy things that he puts you through." He touched my arm. "Be careful. I've known lots of men like Scotty Brian, who are like a stick of dynamite with short fuses."

My head bowed, and I looked sideways at people rushing through the lobby, thinking about how to respond.

"He has some good qualities, but I guess I'm the only one who notices them."

We chatted for about five minutes more, and Lenny said, "I have a few errands to run before the afternoon session. It was good seeing and talking to you, Hannah."

"You, too, give Adelai my love."

As he turned and headed toward the doors leading to the parking structure, he twisted his face toward me and said, "Remember what I said, Hannah. Be careful with that man. There's no telling what he might do."

Scotty's cane nearly hit Lenny's head when he turned back toward the exit. Lenny leaned back to the right, barely being missed by Scotty's attack. Scotty swung at Lenny again, cursing vociferously, causing a dramatic scene in the hotel lobby.

Lenny stepped back and turned sideways toward the garage exit doors, breathing heavily. He stated in a calm tone as he charged toward the swinging doors, "I just completed six months of anger management classes, and I'm not going to let this fool mess up my program."

Scotty wobbled, almost tumbling to the floor. He balanced himself and leaned on one of the hotel towers.

Lenny gazed at me, shaking his head from side to side.

"I feel sorry for you, Hannah. I'm out of here."

Scotty yelled curse words as Lenny marched away. Scotty was so infuriated and possessed by the jealous spirit that he forgot he had bad hips and knees. He tried to run after Lenny, but he lost his balance and fell to the floor. Scotty continued threatening and ranting as he lay on the floor, leaning on one elbow.

Many hotel guests turned and went in opposite directions when they spotted Scotty on the floor shouting, but a few kind men reached out their hands to help him up.

Scotty shouted obscenities at them. "I don't need your help! I can get up on my own! Just get out of my way! Give me my cane!"

One of the gentlemen picked up the cane and handed it to him. Scotty snatched the club from his hand without offering thanks. While Scotty gripped the cane, Lenny stopped at the swinging doors and looked back, his eyes meeting mine. He stared at me as Scotty continued his angry rant, bowed his head, and strode through the swinging doors.

My shoulders slumped, and I shrunk into myself, avoiding eye contact with anyone who glanced in my direction.

Scotty called me every name, but a child of God, as Lenny disappeared through the doors. "You slut! You're supposed to be at a conference, and you're here with that dog. Too bad I don't have my piece with me. We'll finish this discussion at home."

But he didn't wait until we were home. The demonic spirits of jealousy and anger possessed him, and he could not control himself.

As Scotty struggled to rise from the floor, he shouted, "I can't leave you alone for a second. Otherwise, you're picking up some man.

That's why I don't trust you! You don't deserve my trust! I've been waiting for you to earn my respect and trust by acting like a lady, not a tramp. You are worse than an animal! I bet you've been sneaking around seeing that dude after we got married. You're not staying at this hotel because you probably weren't at a conference anyway. You're going home with me now!" He finally took in a breath. "That was a lie, just like everything else you do!"

He grabbed an armchair for support, but it flipped over as he leaned on it. He swore loudly and shouted, "Help me up from this floor! You're the reason that I'm down here anyway."

Too embarrassed and ashamed to speak or move, I blinked back stinging tears, staring at the swinging doors Lenny had gone through and then at the double doors on the opposite side. Ignoring Scotty's demands, feigning deafness, I half walked, half jogged toward the double doors as Scotty threatened. Tears now sprinted down my face.

"Where are you going? Come back here! You ...."

Before he could finish his sentence, I trotted through the first set of doors, praying in the spirit and asking God for peace and protection.

Before stepping onto the street from a second pair of doors, I jerked around to see if Scotty was up and following. The hotel security pulled him up from the floor as I went through the gates onto the outside. I sighed in relief as I strolled, not knowing where I wanted to go. I was just happy to be out of the lion's mouth temporarily.

Scotty was arrested for disorderly conduct and spent the weekend in the county jail. He telephoned multiple times and left messages for me to come to pick him up. A spirit of depression jumped on me, and I spent the weekend in bed crying and eating.

After spending the weekend crying, eating, and putting myself down, I called Dr. Joyce on Monday to seek her input. I relayed every detail of the hotel incident and asked if I had handled the situation appropriately by leaving.

Dr. Joyce hesitated before answering. "I think that you acted wisely. Proverbs 9: 7 (RSV) says,

"He who corrects a scoffer gets himself abuse, and he who reproves a wicked man incurs injury."

It also says in the wisdom book,

> *"The way of a fool is right in his own eyes, but a wise man listens to advice. The vexation of a fool is known at once, but the prudent man ignores an insult"* Proverbs 12: 15-16 (RSV).

And,

> *"He who is slow to anger is better than the mighty, and he who rules his spirit than he who takes a city"* Proverbs 16: 32 (RSV).

After sniffing a few times, I said, "I was so embarrassed and ashamed of allowing him to talk to me like that." I wiped my nose with a tissue. "All of the people staring and shaking their heads."

Dr. Joyce added, "I understand. But you handled it wisely. You didn't stoop to his level and fight in a public establishment. You left the situation, which was most likely the safest thing for you."

I exhaled deeply as if holding my breath. "Thank you for listening and always being available when I need you."

"You are most welcome." She paused and continued, "Hannah, you must make some important decisions. It has to be what's best for you and no one else."

"I know," I said softly.

Dr. Joyce suggested some books I should read, and we hung up.

On Monday afternoon, Moses bailed Scotty out. By Monday evening, the angry spirit had departed, and Scotty was docile when I walked into the house from work. He had cooked dinner, washed dishes, and a dozen red roses smiled from the center of the dining room table. My white delicates, blouses, and slacks were folded and stacked on the bed. We ate dinner in silence, and neither discussed the hotel incident.

During those years with Scotty, I matured spiritually. I didn't want to go through the hell on earth that I went through, but I may not have grown to a more spiritual level if I had not experienced the tribulations, trials, heartaches, disappointments, and headaches.

When I realized my mother was aware of my marital problems, I shared with her more, and she encouraged me each time I complained.

After sharing the Marriott incident with Mom, she said, "You sometimes have to go through to get to."

I thought about her words, agreed with her, and asked God for the strength to go through so I could obtain what Yahweh had stored up for me.

After the incident at the Marriott, we never saw Lenny again. He and Adelai relocated to Minnesota a month after the incident. And when they visited Madison, both avoided Scotty, like preventing a virus from attacking. I missed laughing with Lenny and Adelai. They had been such good friends, and I lost that friendship because of insecurity and unwillingness to stand up for what I believed in – friendship.

I reflected on how the foolishness started - why I stayed in the madness, how it almost destroyed me and Adelai's friendship. My eyes moistened, and I covered my eyes with my hand, remembering how it slaughtered me and Lenny's friendship and how Scotty's craziness almost caused Lenny to go to prison.

A slow, loud sigh escaped. I mumbled, "I don't blame Lenny and Adelai for getting as far away from us as possible."

HONESTY AND DECEPTION

After the hotel encounter, suspicion and surprise rose inside me when Scotty started preparing meals. He had done it before we married but had done absolutely nothing to assist me around the house after marriage. Half his days were with Moses operating their medical equipment business and transportation vans. The other time, he volunteered with the youth group at church, assisted one of his female friends with a task, or spent his time in the bedroom chatting with Charlessa.

After Scotty refused to stop buying presents for his female friends, I quit my part-time job at the school. I still worked full-time at my entrepreneurial endeavor and part-time at the hospital every other weekend. Scotty said since I had quit one of my jobs, I could handle all of the household tasks, inside and outside, without his assistance.

Therefore, I was surprised when I walked inside the house after a hectic and stressful day at work and sniffed a heavenly aroma. "Wow, it smells good in here. What has the house smelling so good?"

Scotty smiled and kissed me on the lips. "I felt like cooking today and made you a special meal."

"Well, it sure smells wonderful." I started peeping in pots, looked in the oven door, and looked in the refrigerator to see what we would have for beverages.

"I made meatloaf with turkey and beef since you're trying to stop eating pork, a seven-layer salad, green beans with potatoes and sweet onions, potato salad, and lemon crème pie for dessert."

He stood straight and tall, his face beaming with pride when I glanced at him. It reminded me of the Scotty that made me fall for him. The caring gentleman who stood in the doorway until I was safely in my car. The man who cleaned the snow off of my car before I went to work. My knight who limped in the rain or snow to bring the car and pick me up at the doorway so I wouldn't get wet. My bodyguard who peeped through the blinds or stood in the yard until I was safely in the house when arriving home at midnight.

My body warmed, and a sense of the old love we had surfaced. "This is so special, Scotty. I had a stressful day today, and this is making me feel better already. Thank you." I wanted to ask what prompted him to prepare dinner but decided against it. Scotty was calm, non-argumentative, and loving, and the tranquility was enjoyable. I wanted to relish the moment.

We talked and ate without one disagreement, a miracle in itself. Afterward, Scotty started preparing dinner daily. He used precooked meatloaf, Salisbury steak, or chicken entrees, loaded with high fats and calories. Because he was trying to help out a little bit, I didn't want to complain. I told myself to eat only one Salisbury steak, one slice of meatloaf, or one piece of chicken and not to eat dessert at all.

But I would be so hungry when I walked into the house that my conversation with myself went out the window. I ate double portions of everything, including dessert. As I think back, I'm sure the stress had something to do with my overeating. Even though Scotty tried to argue less at home, his glares, frowns, or fake smiles when I talked to others told a different story.

Four times a week, we ate high-fat, high-calorie meals.

Not surprisingly, my weight swelled to 250 pounds. Because I worked out every day on the treadmill or bike, I was toned and deceived myself into thinking I didn't look like I weighed that much. To camouflage the weight, I started wearing suits with long blazers that covered my hips and stomach and layered or pleated tops that hid the excess weight.

Since Scotty picked out most of my clothing, which was one size too large anyway, I got used to wearing my clothes more oversized. With skirts to my ankles, blouses buttoned to my neck, and pants with elastic waist, I honestly didn't pay much attention to the weight gain.

Before marriage, Scotty bought bright-colored clothing for me, but after marriage, he purchased only black or dark clothes - black pantsuits, dresses, suits, sportswear, and outerwear. I assumed he bought the dark clothing because he thought it made me look slimmer.

I didn't realize that those drab, dark, morbid, lifeless, black clothes were draining my energy and making me act older than my forty-plus years. Before getting involved with Scotty, I had always worn bright, lively, energetic colors. I believe he bought all-black clothing because he dealt with the occult. Black is associated with the devil, evil, fear, and death. Black usually has a negative connotation – most people still wear black to a funeral, and most symbols of witches and warlocks have them wearing black. A black cat crossing the street in front of you is supposed to be bad luck, and the signs of the devil usually have him wearing black.

After getting bigger and bigger and bigger each year, I finally acknowl-edged that I had gained over 100 pounds since being with Scotty.

At a shopping event with my sisters, I pouted and frowned because I couldn't find anything in the size I thought I was. The others were finding great bargains, and I couldn't find anything to fit me in the styles they selected. After trying on multiple skirts, slacks, blouses, and suits, to my disappointment and shock, nothing fit. I could not pull the slacks or skirts over my hips or button the blouses.

Because I walked every day and looked well in my clothes, I didn't think I had gained that much weight. When Elana brought a size twenty and said, "Try this one, Hannah," I glared at her.

I flipped the dress around. "I am not that big. How about a six-teen-wide?"

Elana's eyes widened, and her brows creased. "Hannah, you can't wear a sixteen or eighteen."

The tears tried to come, but I valiantly fought them. "I am not wearing a size twenty." I studied my body in the three-way mirror.

Elana studied my body as if willing me to wear a smaller size. "What do you want me to do?"

I am not moving up to a size twenty. Have I doubled in size from ten to twenty?

"I'll come out and look for myself," I said. After Elana moved away, the tears won and dripped down my cheeks while I sat in the dressing room, trying to pull myself together. I couldn't believe I had let myself go like that and not taken better care of my body by eating nutritiously and healthier.

At that moment, I decided to eat healthier and exercise more vigorously. And the seesaw of losing weight and gaining more back started. For a week or two, I ate healthier, then slipped back into my old habits of eating dessert nightly, eating in bed, and eating double portions. My weight loss effort was like a yo-yo, weight down with multiple diets and pounds back up when I relapsed.

Whenever I read of a new diet, I told myself that's what I was missing and subjected my body to another torturous eating plan. Five pounds would drop from one of the many diets, but when I got upset with Scotty or became depressed, or didn't think I was losing weight fast enough, I would cry, whine, and give up. "Forget it! I might as well eat what I want. I'm not losing weight anyway."

And I would gain an extra five pounds when I went off the diet plan. I now realize that was the voice of Satan deceiving me to continue with my unhealthy, detrimental eating style. Lucifer manipulated me into destroying my body with the up-and-down weight changes. Satan wants to destroy us in any way that he can. I must admit that he is smart enough to stick with what works. His method of deception has not changed. He twists what God has said to make you second-guess Yahweh's voice. He also causes you to second-guess yourself. The devil tempts you with a spirit of pride or self-pity. Then you're with him temporarily. He deceived me with the moods of pride and self-pity, but he was trying to destroy me with gluttony.

As I said, I gained ten to fifteen pounds more after getting off the diet. Each time I went off of a diet, I was heavier than before I started, and losing the excess weight became harder and harder.

While mutilating my body with regular diets and erratic weight changes, medical problems also emerged from the excess weight and the up again, down again weight changes. The weight gain took my blood pressure out of control. It was primarily due to the stress from my relationship with Scotty. But gaining over a hundred pounds didn't help the situation. After discovering that several of my relatives had diabetes, I realized I was also making myself a prime target for that disease if I didn't lose weight and start taking better care of myself.

Instead of supporting me, Scotty made fun of me and condemned me for not having discipline. At family gatherings at my house, he shamed me by bringing attention to the food on my plate or that I made a third visit to the food line. I stopped inviting my family to our home, which was perhaps his purpose.

During a Thanksgiving gathering, Scotty stood behind me while I ate at the dining room table with my mother and sisters. "Hey y'all, Hannah lost five pounds, but she found them today."

The men laughed, thinking it funny and that Scotty was joking and not attempting to demoralize me. My mother and sisters looked at me compassionately and quickly changed the conversation to 'Black Friday' shopping.

SEEING BUT NOT BELIEVING

Other dubious things started happening as we headed into the second year of our marriage.

The first thing that grabbed my attention was puzzling phone calls. The phone rang when I walked into the house, but the caller hung up when I answered. It was like someone knew exactly when I strolled into the house. Later in the evening, when I answered the telephone, heavy breathing sounded on the other end, but the caller said nothing. Oddly, a conversation ensued with the caller whenever Scotty answered the phone.

I broached the topic several times with him, and Scotty accused me of being suspicious each time. He said, "It's all in your mind, Hannah. No one's calling this house and hanging up or not saying anything. Why is someone always on the line when I answer, and no one is there when you answer? Unless it's a signal you two have; he doesn't say anything until you signal that I'm not home."

My mouth opened, and the back of my head dropped to my neck. "That doesn't make any sense." A purposeful, loud sigh fell from my lips. "If I had signals set up with someone, I wouldn't be complaining. Strangely, the caller always talks when you answer the phone. I say the calls are for you, and they don't want to talk to me." I added, "If it's one of your lady friends, tell them it is common courtesy to acknowledge the lady of the house when you call her home."

"Who says you're a lady? Maybe they don't say anything because there is no *lady* of the house to acknowledge." He chuckled. "I'm not saying that anyone is calling. I still think it's all in your crazy little head. But if it were true, that could be the reason."

"Oh, well. Can you tell the caller that it's disrespectful to call someone's house and not at least say, "Hello, may I speak to Scotty?"

He smirked, entered the bedroom, closed the door, and started chatting with someone on the landline.

After the suspicious phone calls started, eerie feelings crept through me that someone was stalking us. Similar to Scotty's tailing me before we married when he recovered at my home after his hip surgery. Now more aware if a vehicle stayed behind me for longer than a mile since Scotty's stalking. I watched for strange cars parked at the corner or the same automobile driving past my house. I suspected someone was spying on us when I spotted a green Ford model car pause in front of our property and drive off when I walked onto the porch.

Because we lived in a cul-de-sac, we rarely had excessive traffic driving past our home. While I was on vacation and relaxing on the deck, my curiosity peaked when I noticed more traffic than usual. After paying attention, I realized it was the same automobile. I wasn't sure if the driver was male or female or if more than one person was in the car since the windows were tinted dark. Not being very automobile literate, I couldn't identify the model of the car. As the vehicle sped away, I spotted the Ford name but couldn't read if it was a Focus, Taurus, Fusion, or Mustang.

Sometimes the cars flicked their headlights as they passed the house. I'm unsure if that meant anything because Scotty didn't do anything differently if he was home.

The cruising persisted for weeks and suddenly ceased after a young female knocked on my door and said she heard that our house was for sale and was interested in listing it. I informed her that the house was not for sale and asked who told her the property was on the market. She evaded my question, gave me a card with a real estate name and phone number, and asked me to call her first if I decided to sell my home.

For a moment, the spirits of anger and disgust overcame me, my eyes squinting and nose crinkling. After slamming the door shut, I ripped the card and threw it in the trash. "If I sell my home, it won't be to you. Some nerve; to ring my doorbell and ask if my house was for sale. Did she see a for sale sign on the lawn? No!" The veins in my neck throbbed, and my face heated.

Later in the evening, I regretted tearing the card up. I wanted to call and find out if the visitor was a legitimate real estate agent, or if it was a disconnected number, or a private residence.

Before retiring for bed, I asked Scotty if he knew a young, attractive female real estate agent. "She stopped by today and said she heard I was selling my property."

Scotty looked at me, appalled. "Of course, I know real estate agents. You aren't the only one that's owned a home. I've owned several homes and used real estate agents to sell and buy homes."

"Did you tell that lady that we were selling my home? Did you put my house on the market?"

"Of course not; it's your house and not mine to sell!"

I never found out if it was another one of his games, tricking me into thinking there was a market for my home so I'd sell it. My gut tells me she was one of Scotty's gift-receiving females who wanted to see what Scotty's wife looked like or what type of house we lived in.

Of course, Scotty was not mindful of Ford model cars patrolling our cul-de-sac and didn't observe any more traffic than we usually had. He said it was all in my mind and denied seeing any unfamiliar vehicles. I wasn't a total nitwit, even though Scotty thought I was.

Afterward, the same green Ford tailed us when we exited the cul-de-sac. On our way to a Saturday breakfast, I monitored the green car in my sideview mirror as it pulled behind us. "What type of car is the green one behind us?" I asked in a sugary voice.

Scotty glanced in his rearview mirror. "It looks like a Ford Taurus. You like that car?"

"No, it's an ugly green," I hesitated and added, "I think that Taurus is following us. It looks like the same car that stopped in front of our house but drove off when I opened the front door."

Scotty's head shook. "Get your mind out of the gutter and stop being so scared of everything. No one is following us." He twisted his face toward me. "Unless some dude is following you." His eyes narrowed as he smirked.

As an afterthought, he asked, "Why would anyone be following us, Hannah?"

"I don't know." My shoulders shrugged. "Maybe your friend wants more than a friendship." *Or you already have more than a friendship, and she wants to discover how much time you spent with me*, I thought. *And I'm ninety-nine percent positive one of your female friends is stalking us.*

The stoplight turned green, but Scotty froze and stared at me with wide eyes as if in shock.

"The light is green, sweetheart," I said.

Scotty switched the radio on, and we drove the rest of the way to the restaurant listening to sports radio.

The following Saturday, we went to Whole Foods after breakfast to pick up a few items. Scotty loved grocery shopping, so we spent about an hour or so in the store. He stopped at the fruit and vegetable areas, tasting samples and inspecting fruits and vegetables. From the corner of my eyes, I glimpsed a tall, shapely, young, attractive female standing behind us, waiting to sample the melon.

"Is it sweet?" she asked, smiling at me.

I returned the smile. "I haven't tasted it yet. Is the melon sweet, Scotty?"

He scowled, avoiding eye contact with the young lady.

"Taste it! What's sweet to me may not be sweet to you." He pushed the cart away from the melons. "Let's go look at the cucumbers."

I glanced at the woman and then nodded toward the melons, a close-lipped smile on my face.

Scotty picked out cucumbers, tomatoes, and fresh corn on the cob, and we headed toward the deli. Sensing someone was staring at us, I glanced to the left peripherally, and the once-smiling female now scowled as she stared at us. "I wonder why that young lady is staring at us like that."

"That lady is not staring at us. You're imagining things again, Hannah."

"How do you know? You weren't even looking in her direction. I sensed someone watching us, glanced back, and she was gawking at us."

"Well, I have no idea why she was *gawking* at us. She was probably looking at the fresh fish or the deli, and you just thought she was looking at you. Why would she be looking at you? Are you trying to tell me women are attracted to you now?"

There he goes again, trying to make me the culprit. "I didn't say she was gawking at me. I said she was staring at *us*. Maybe she remembers you from the organizations you are involved with, or maybe she was Charlessa's friend. I bet she's trying to remember where she knows you from."

"What concern is it to you who the lady is? I really didn't pay any attention to her. If she was one of Charlessa's friends, I'm sure she would have introduced herself. Forget it, Hannah. Let's go see what types of cakes they have."

The tall, shapely, attractive young lady with black hair in a short bob popped up on every aisle we went. I studied her caramel oval face as she strolled toward us on the bread aisle. She entered a lane shortly after Scotty and me, read ingredients on products, and loitered until we left. Soon afterward, she'd be on the same aisle as us. While glancing at her several times, I hoped to make eye contact, but she didn't acknowledge me.

Finally, after an hour and a half, Scotty, leaning on the cart for support, pushed our buggy to the checkout. The same lady strolled to a checkout stand adjacent to us and paid for her one small bag of groceries. "Look, Scotty, there she is again." My head nodded in the woman's direction. "She has been in this store for one and a half hours and only bought one small bag of groceries. That lady was following us. I don't care what you say. She watched us here." She was so young and attractive that it never entered my mind she may have been watching Scotty for personal reasons. In his past, Scotty had crossed so many people I assumed he had told her off when he was in one of his obnoxious moods.

Scotty mumbled something under his breath and growled. "Grab those last two bags, and let's get out of here."

The shopper fumbled inside her bag as if looking for an item until we headed toward the exit. As we passed the station, she bumped into Scotty, her face still gazing into her shopping bag. She fluttered her eyelids as she glanced up at him. "Oh, I'm so sorry."

"No problem," said Scotty, standing straighter and leaning less on the grocery cart.

She smiled and tilted her head toward Scotty, rubbing hair behind her left ear. "You're the man who wouldn't tell me if the melons were sweet, " she said.

Scotty kept heading toward the exit doors, not desiring to converse with the woman.

I smiled. "Did you taste the melons? Were they sweet?"

"They were scrumptious." She pointed to her bag. "I bought one."

When I glanced up, Scotty was going through the exit doors. "I'd better catch up with my husband."

When I reached the car, Scotty threw his bags into the back seat. He slid behind the steering wheel, staring at a man pushed in a wheelchair. He shook his head, saying, "I don't ever want to be in that situation." He nodded toward the gentleman in the wheelchair. "I pray I never become incapacitated and need someone to care for me." His eyes darted in my direction. "You'd probably put me in a nursing home in a heartbeat."

My head replied, "Yes, I would." But my mouth stayed closed, watching him study the disabled gentleman.

PRIDE BEFORE DISASTER

I began believing that the many perilous activities that happened while I was with Scotty occurred because I disobeyed God and gave in to Scotty rather than obeying Jevohah. Our pastors frequently stated that God is a forgiving and merciful God, and we suffer consequences for our sinful and disobedient behaviors. My husband's stubbornness and evil behaviors had no end, and I suffered tremendous consequences by yoking with an unbeliever.

In mid-January, during winter break, while taking my grandson, Desmond, up north to computer camp, Scotty missed a turn and drove in the wrong direction for two hours. He wouldn't stop and ask for advice.

"There's an exit coming up, Scotty. Let's get off, find a service station, and ask for directions."

"We're not lost. If we keep driving, we'll run back into Interstate 94."

"We've been driving for an hour, and I haven't seen any signs for Eau Clare. I think we're going in the wrong direction. Let's pull off at the next exit and get directions to ensure we're going the right way." He didn't respond and drove past the next exit.

"If I'm reading this map right," I said, "we are almost near Minnesota. I keep seeing I-90. Shouldn't we be on I-94?"

Before he answered, I said, "We are going in the wrong direction. Scotty?" He kept his eyes on the road and didn't reply.

"Did you hear me?"

He mumbled something under his breath. Thirty minutes later, he said, "You don't know how to read a map. You're probably looking at the wrong landmarks. Give me the map."

"You can't drive and read a map at the same time. Let's pull off at the next exit, and you can tell me if I was reading the map wrong."

He exited and pulled into a service station lot, snatched the map from my lap, studied it, and got out of the car. "I've got to go to the restroom."

I watched him and the service station attendant look at a map, with the attendant pointing toward the direction we had come from. Scotty said nothing as he got back in the car.

"Were we going in the wrong direction? Do we now have to backtrack for two hours? That's four hours of lost time."

"Stop complaining. You're not driving. I must have missed the interstate somewhere back there. We'll get Desmond to camp in time for check-in."

By the time we got to camp, settled Desmond in, and headed back home to Madison, it was past 7:00 p.m. A black night sky replaced the hazy, gray day heavens.

Because of Scotty's arrogance, a three-hour trip took us seven hours. Snow drifted from the sky as we started home. We thought we could make the three-hour drive before the snow became too heavy and visibility impaired.

We had driven for ninety minutes and made excellent time when the snow started raining down out of nowhere. It was difficult to spot the red taillights of the vehicle in front of us, the large white flakes stuck to the windshield like leaches - heavy, wet snow. The wiper blades roared to push the snow from the window. A violent sputtering sound came from underneath the car. Lights flashed on the dashboard, and the engine was dying, like a wounded pig taking its last breath. The vehicle stopped on us in the middle of nowhere. Scotty steered the car off of the interstate highway onto the shoulder.

It was now 9:00 p.m., and the country area we docked in had no streetlights on the interstate. I buttoned my coat, wrapped a scarf around my neck, and slid on mittens. My body acted as if the temperature was zero degrees or below. With no streetlights or headlights, the darkness was so thick I thought I could cut through it with a knife. We discussed if we should wait for assistance or try walking to find an open service station, listing the pros and cons of staying in the car or going for help.

"Someone will pass by eventually," I insisted. "I think the highway patrol passes by every hour or so."

"But what if they don't and no one drives by? I'm not going to freeze in this car. Try calling 911 and see if we can get a tow truck out here."

I pulled out my cell phone and dialed 911, and the numbers didn't punch. *What's wrong with this phone?* I flicked on the interior light and looked at the mobile, and the battery was dead. "It says the battery is dead and won't let me dial 911."

"Well, plug it in the lighter and recharge it!" He said, his nose creasing upward.

I opened the glove compartment, reached for the phone charger, and didn't feel it. I pulled everything out, and still no charger. *It has to be in here. I always keep an extra one in the glove compartment. Where is it?* "It's not in here. Maybe it's with the CDs and cassette tapes."

After pulling out the cassette tapes, CDs, and no phone charger, my breath quickened. *Where could it be?* "I can't find the phone charger. I can't call 911." I nibbled my bottom lip. "I always keep one in the glove compartment but can't find it. Where is your cell phone?"

"In the pocket of the jacket I had on before we left home." Being the macho man, Scotty struggled out of the car and started walking back the way we had come, saying he remembered seeing a gas station exit a few miles back.

Suspecting it would take him hours to walk two miles with his bad hips, knees, and a cane, if he made it at all, I thought *I could be frozen or have frostbite by the time he got back.* "Why don't I walk back? I can walk faster," I volunteered, and then quickly added, "Not that you couldn't do it, Scotty, but with the snow and your cane, it would probably take you longer."

After trudging a mile back to the service station, it was closed. I pounded on the door, hoping someone might still be inside. "Thank God I wore my snow boots," I mumbled as I tramped and pounded on the back door—still silent. I inhaled and exhaled several times while rubbing my hands together. My fingers and toes were losing sensation, getting numb from the cold. *I might as well head back to the car.* With the snow dropping like quail from heaven, I lumbered the mile back to our vehicle, frustrated, freezing, cold, wet, scared, and praying:

> *For the Spirit that God gave us is no cowardly spirit, but one to inspire power, love, and self-discipline* II Timothy 1: 7 (REV).

I asked God for protection, warmth, and help. As a blur of our car came into view, the Holy Spirit reminded me that I had blankets, extra clothes, and socks in the car's trunk. He also told me to call 911 from the cell phone again. *But I already tried that, and the battery is dead.*

The voice whispered again while taking the blankets, clothes, and socks out of the trunk. *Call 911 from your cell phone.* Rubbing my hands together to warm them up because my fingers were too numb to press the numbers, I punched **9-1-1** and was routed to a local sheriff. I explained our situation.

The Sheriff said, "We're pretty backed up with accidents and people in ditches, but I'll send someone to Interstate East 94 as soon as a van is available. It's rough out there. The tow trucks are even getting stuck."

"We couldn't call towing because my phone died, and I don't have my charger. You can send Triple AAA if they can make it here."

"We have special vehicles and tires that can handle this weather. Well, bundle up in blankets and cuddle together. You'll stay warmer. And someone will be at your location as soon as they can."

We sat in the car for another hour, wrapped in our separate blankets, waiting for the patrol van. I jogged in place in my seat, trying to keep my blood circulating.

Finally, I said, "We've been sitting for an hour and no highway patrol. I think I'll have more circulation walking than sitting in this cold car. I will walk in the other direction to see if I can find a service station open, a home, or some visible lights."

Cold and shivering, I started plodding to find help. The snow was so wet and deep. Each step was like moving in quicksand; the snow was so weighty. It was now higher than my boots, and my clothes were soaked to the waist. My pants were soaked before I made it twelve feet from the car.

After falling three times in fifteen minutes and still able to eyeball the car, I gave up and headed back. "It's awful out there! I fell three times and couldn't walk in the heavy, slippery snow. We'll have to pray and believe that the sheriff will send somebody soon and not forget about us." I changed into the dry clothes I'd taken from the trunk.

Around 2:00 a.m., after waiting five hours for rescue and being unsuccessful in my attempts to walk for help, an Amish couple with their four children came down the highway. We flagged them down, shouted that we needed help, and asked if they could take us to the nearest open service station.

The husband stopped the buggy, handed the reins to his wife, climbed down, and walked over to our car. Scotty and I stood next to our vehicle. The bearded man smiled, said his name was Ishmael, and asked about our problem. We explained what had happened and that we needed transportation to the nearest service station to call a towing service.

Ishmael apologized and explained that he knew nothing about automobiles and couldn't assist us but would take us to the nearest service station about two miles up the road south.

Scotty's face twisted toward me. "Two miles up the road, south! If you had kept walking instead of turning around, you would have been at the service station by now, Hannah."

I didn't respond. *Didn't he see me fall multiple times and how difficult it was to navigate the snow?* A second thought came. *Scotty might be right; I should've tried harder instead of giving up. Something kept telling me to keep going south, but I was too afraid I would fight the snow for two to three miles and not find a service station open like I did when I went north, and then have to walk another three miles back to the car in all of the snow.*

A nervous stirring in my spirit tried to make me guilty and angry at myself for not forging through the snow. I had had this feeling many times and knew it was not of God. I also realized if I didn't bind the emotion, it would make me depressed. *Please help me be more discerning of your voice, to stop, pause, and listen carefully before making a decision.* A calm, peaceful presence encircled me, and God answered my prayer, whispering, "Daughter, you wouldn't have made it." The feelings of guilt and anger left.

Scotty suggested that I stay in the car, and he'd go with the family to the service station since the buggy did not have enough room for both of us. "Wrap up in the blankets and keep the doors locked. I'll return when the tow truck arrives at the service station."

"My hands and feet are numb, Scotty. Let me go with them, and I can warm up inside the service station while waiting for the tow truck."

"You stay here! I think you'll be safer here."

"You think I'll be safer alone in the middle of nowhere, in pitch black darkness, getting frostbite? That doesn't make sense, Scotty."

The family sat without talking, listening to our conversation, waiting for us to decide which one would take the ride to the service station.

"You're so argumentative, Hannah! What if the service station is not open? What if thugs or hoodlums are hanging around? What would you do with them?"

"At 2:00 a. m.? I don't think any thugs will be out in the middle of nowhere this morning and in this weather." I sighed. "Go ahead. I'll stay in the car. But please come back as fast as you can. I am shivering from the cold, and my fingers and toes are numb."

Scotty hoisted himself on the buggy and sat beside one of the children with his legs hanging, his feet almost touching the ground.

I tramped across the street, jumped back in the car, locked the doors, and wrapped my feet in one blanket and my upper body and hands in Scotty's blanket. My body trembled from the extreme cold. The buggy pulled onto the highway and trotted away. The small taillights disappeared in the darkness.

I wrapped the blankets around my upper and lower body, rubbing my hands together to warm them and patting my feet to keep the circulation moving, my body shivering. Time crept like a colossal tortoise slowly crawling back into a pond. I sang to keep myself occupied, played hide and seek with the stars, and looked for the different galaxies in the sky as I waited for Scotty to return.

Hunger pains stabbed me. I searched my purse for a candy bar, mints, or snack crackers. My stomach growled and ached. *Boy, I should be hungry.* I hadn't eaten anything since breakfast. I found a Snickers bar and grabbed it so quickly that I spilled the contents of my purse. A bright yellow and orange package dropped to the floor. *What's this?*

I picked up the bright-colored bag, and it said hand warmers. "Thank you, Jesus! These warmers are a blessing from you."

My sister, Tarrin, had given me the gloves for Christmas and told me to try them when I was outside for long periods. She was into winter sports, like ice skating and skiing, and always gave me some new items to try after she had used them and thought they were effective.

Three pairs of warmers fell out of the packet. I slipped a couple into my boots to warm my feet, and another two I attached to my mittens to heat my hands. "Ah, that heat feels good. Shoot, I've got to take my gloves off to take the wrapper off my candy bar."

After snatching the wrapping off of the Snickers bar, I took a huge bite and slid my hands back into the mittens attached to the hand warmers. "Ooh, that heat feels so good on my hands and feet."

A bit warmer and more comfortable with the warmers, I dozed off. I jumped when Scotty and the tow truck arrived around 3:30 a.m. At the same time, a snowplow and salt truck swished past, pushing the snow from the interstate away from our vehicle. Sprinkling salt lay where at least four feet of snow had been minutes before.

The mechanic hooked the cables up and recharged the battery on our car, thinking the battery had died in this cold weather. After the recharge, the car started but went silent once he removed the battery cables. He charged the battery twice, and each time the vehicle stopped running when he pulled the wires. He scratched his head and looked at the battery, puzzled, then walked to the driver's side door, opened it, and looked at the dashboard. He sloshed back to the front of the car, looked under the hood, reconnected the cables, and recharged the battery a third time. He slid behind the steering wheel and switched the ignition on as the battery charged. "You people have run out of gas. I can tow you to the service station or bring you a few gallons of gas back."

"Why don't you just bring a couple of gallons of gas back, and we can make it to the gas station and fill up," Scotty replied.

As the tow truck drove away, I expected Scotty to blame me for us running out of gas. I waited for him to say I should have filled the car before we got on the road. To my surprise, he slid into the car, sat behind the steering wheel, and said nothing.

The tow truck driver returned and poured the gasoline into the tank. "You don't have to pay me for the gasoline. I feel sorry for you folks, being out here since 9:00 p.m. yesterday."

We made it to the gas station, and I went inside to warm up while Scotty filled the gas tank. The ride home was silent.

The following morning, my hands and feet blistered. Scotty took me to the emergency room, where the doctor diagnosed me with a mild case of frostbite. The physician didn't think I would have any permanent damage to my tissues, saying, "You're fortunate you had the hand warmers and smart enough to put them on your feet and hands. The warmers sufficiently warmed your hands and feet to increase circulation and prevent internal damage."

"Thank God," I said. "It's a miracle I didn't lose fingers, toes, or an extremity."

Scotty showed no signs of frostbite or skin damage from the cold.

STILETTO HEELS

I wouldn't have kept my sanity if it hadn't been for loving and caring family and friends. Even when I avoided them, my sisters or friends would pop up, take me out, and make me laugh.

I didn't attend gatherings with Shirley or Michelle for the first year of my marriage, telling them I had other engagements. I was surprised when Shirley called out of the blue and told me she and Michelle were taking me out for my birthday, and she was not taking no for an answer. "Tell Scotty we're taking you out on May 1, so you will be available for him on your birthday, May 5th. No excuses. We'll pick you up at 5:00 p.m."

At 5:00 p.m., May 1, Shirley and Michelle were blowing the horn for me to leave my house. Fighting the grin on the inside, trying to move outside, I threw my jacket over my shoulder and told Scotty the time I expected to be home.

He didn't look up from the television but said, "Uh huh."

As I opened the door to the porch, I said, "I'll call if we're running late," and rushed out to the waiting car.

Grins covered Shirley and Michelle's faces as they waved. Shirley said in her bossy tone, "Hop in the back because I'm not moving for you to sit in the front. I know you don't like to ride in the back seat."

I responded while I slid into the back. "Queens ride in the back anyway. Hey ladies, I am so happy to be with you." They updated me on their families as we drove to the restaurant.

When we reached the restaurant, I was overjoyed to see Adelai waiting to celebrate my birthday. We laughed, reminisced, and talked about our families and our men. I shared some weird things Scotty had started doing after his daughter's death.

"How is everything going in your marriage?" asked Michelle.

All six eyes focused on me. I avoided eye contact, and my voice slightly stammered as I shared heartfelt emotions with my friends. "As I said, he's been acting weird since Charlessa's death and started seeing a psychic." I shuffled food around on my plate. "He threatened me with a butcher knife during one of our arguments."

"No way," Michelle said.

"What happened?" asked Shirley.

Adelai was quiet, and when I glanced at her, she bowed her head, her mouth straight.

I continued. "Scotty was slicing a cantaloupe and complaining of what a bad wife I was, that his life was worse since he married me, we had a miserable marriage, and he had less now than before he married me. I was sitting at the table and said he should find another place to live if he was *so* unhappy and his life was *so* miserable. Before I realized it, he pointed the knife toward my chest and said he would cut my heart out if I said something like that again."

Shirley and Michelle gasped, and Adelai's hands went to her heart.

"I wasn't afraid. I had this unbelievable boldness and thought if it was my time to go, it was my day to depart this earth. I did not show fear. The demonic spirits sensed the spirits of faith and power emanating from me and consented to the *power* of the Holy Spirit. I stared directly into his eyes as he pointed the knife at my chest. I used wisdom, of course, and didn't do or say anything to provoke him. I didn't argue with him, and he went back to slicing the melon as though nothing had happened."

"That would have scared me to death," Michelle exclaimed.

"We would still be fighting if Markus pulled a stunt like that," said Shirley.

Adelai just looked at me, shook her head, and said she couldn't believe I was going through that with him. "You deserve better than that, Hannah. You're the one who always reminded us that we were royalty and deserved to be treated as queens and princesses. What happened to you? Why are you settling for less than what God has for you?"

"I loved Scotty when we married and honestly believed the jealousy and control would leave after I was his wife. He has good qualities, but the negative ones suffocate the positives." My voice lowered as I shrugged. "Plus, I'm married to him and trying to make the marriage work. He hasn't committed adultery, so I don't have a legal, biblical reason to divorce him."

"That's not true," Shirley interjected. "Physical, verbal, emotional, and even sexual abuse are all valid reasons for a divorce biblically. God doesn't want us in chaos, confusion, frustration, and being abused by our spouses. Everything isn't spelled out in the Bible—for some issues, you have to pray for discernment and wisdom from the Holy Spirit. There's a scripture that talks about pursuing peace. I can't remember where it is in the Bible now, but if I find it, I'll call you. That scripture tells me that God doesn't want us to be in situations that do not promote peace."

We sat quietly; each lady engrossed in her thoughts until the waitress brought the check and our take-home containers. As we hugged, kissed each other goodbye, and walked to the car, Shirley whispered, "Call me if he does that again, and I'll call the ladies' group, and we'll all come over and show him what it feels like to be abused."

I laughed as we loaded into the car. "Girl, you are too crazy."

A week later, Shirley, Michelle, and my five sisters arrived at my house, all carrying four-inch stiletto heels.

"Is Scotty home?" asked Shirley.

"No. Scotty's at a doctor's appointment, I think. What do you want with him?"

Kameron, my youngest sister, who is usually quiet, spoke up. "Shirley said that Scotty held a butcher knife to your chest. Is that true?"

The veins in Elana's neck ballooned as she questioned. "And why didn't you tell us when we were over last month?"

My middle sister, Ashley, said matter-of-factly, "We came over to tell him that it's unacceptable behavior and to remind him that our mom told him on your wedding day that you were already raised and didn't need a daddy."

"And to beat him with these stilettos," Shirley announced. "Those pointed heels can kill, Hannah."

I looked at their faces to see if they were serious and burst into laughter. With my hands on my thighs, bent over with my head almost to my knees, I leaned on the wall laughing so hard that tears came. Water streamed from my eyes, down my cheeks, and into my chest. I couldn't stop laughing.

"We're serious, Hannah," Shirley said, smiling. Then she cackled. Before long, Elana, Christy, Ashley, Kameron, Tarrin, and Michelle were laughing.

We leaned on each other against the wall, and Shirley slid to the floor on her knees. We laughed until tears flowed from our eyes for what seemed like hours. Every time we stopped laughing, one of them would hold up a stiletto, and we would all start cackling again.

After we belly-laughed until we couldn't laugh anymore, tears fought their way through my eyes, and grief-stricken moans slipped from my mouth. The ladies rushed to comfort me, surrounding and cuddling me like one would support a widow at her husband's funeral.

Elana said while hugging my shoulder, "Hannah, you have too many blood sisters, spiritual sisters, and sister-friends to be in another abusive relationship. We might not use the heels, but we will help you escape from him."

"He, he needs to leave. This is my home...." I stopped in the middle of my sentence.

"What's more important to you, Hannah, this house or your life?" Elana replied.

"I don't think he would kill me. He might hit me because he has a violent past."

"That's what they all say, 'I don't think he will kill me,' until they end up in the hospital or morgue," Shirley interjected.

"I'm not rejecting what you're saying, and I understand you're doing this because you love and care for me. I just don't feel I should leave just yet. I don't sense it in my spirit. I'm always praying for the Holy Spirit's guidance, and I believe the Holy Spirit will inform me when and *if* it is time to leave. I don't believe God will let Scotty do anything to hurt me. I am covered with the Blood of Jesus, and my God is greater than any of the demonic forces living within Scotty."

"Just remember that you are not alone, and we are here for you," said Elana.

"And we've got your back!" Shirley said.

After hugging each other, we ate teacakes I had baked, drank tea and coffee, and sat and talked until Scotty returned home. He stopped in his tracks when he spotted the ladies sitting on the deck. After settling himself, Scotty tried to make small talk and joke with them. The ladies were not interested in chatting with him, so he told them to enjoy their tea and cakes and limped into the house with his cane.

BLACKBIRD

That Saturday, Kameron and Tarrin, the two youngest sisters, called me on a three-way call, laughing and gasping between chuckles as I picked up the phone. "Hannah, you won't believe what happened to us today," Kameron said, laughing between words. "We were held hostage in our apartment by a little blackbird." She started chuckling again.

Tarrin picked up when Kameron stopped giggling. "It wasn't a *little* blackbird. It was a *huge* blackbird!"

"It was not a huge blackbird, Tarrin. It was a baby bird, and we were scared of a little blackbird." Kameron laughed.

Both started laughing as I interjected, "What are you talking about? What blackbird? And where did the bird hold you hostage?" I asked, intrigued.

"I was in the basement doing laundry, and something flew over my head," Kameron replied. "I thought it was a bat, so I screamed, grabbed a chair to fight it, and peeped through the holes in the chair's back. Here was this beautiful, sweet blackbird sitting on the windowsill. "What are you doing in my basement instead of outside," I asked the bird.

When I spoke, the bird dashed up the stairs.

Tarrin interrupted, "I heard pecking on my upstairs door. I thought it was Kam. I opened the door, and this huge black bird flew downstairs."

Laughing again, Kameron said, "It was not huge, Tarrin."

Tarrin chuckled. "Hannah, it was gigantic. It looked like a big crow! Like a flash of lightning, I closed my door and called Kam to tell her a huge bird was flying around in the hallway."

Kameron giggled. "I called my boyfriend and asked him to come over and chase the bird out of my basement, and we had to wait for Bruno to get off work, so me and Tarrin stayed in our apartments all day, scared of a cute, little blackbird. I had so much planned for today, and nothing got done." She chuckled. "You needed to be there to see how funny it was, Hannah."

Tarrin started talking, "When Bruno came to catch the bird, the little creature kept avoiding him. I didn't go down, but that's what Kam said. She said that it seemed like the bird was playing with her boyfriend. It flew to a corner, waited for him to come, and then flew to another corner."

Kam added, "That's right. Bruno put birdseed in a box, and the bird flew above the box, looked in it, and shook its head as to say, "I'm not that stupid, and I'm not that hungry." It flew to another beam in the basement." All three of us laughed then.

"It sounds like that was a smart bird," I replied.

"Tarrin wouldn't come down to help us. She peeped out her door and shouted instructions. It was a brilliant bird. I covered up the side of the door with openings large enough for it to fly through when I thought Bruno had her cornered in the back, and that smart bird flew over his head to the opposite side of the room and found an opening big enough to fly through. Then she flew upstairs and pecked on Tarrin's door again."

"Did you come out and help, Tarrin?" I asked.

"No. I feared the bird would be threatened and cornered and peck me in the face with its beak or little feet."

"Did you finally catch the brilliant little creature?" I breathed into the receiver while waiting for one of them to answer.

Kameron responded, "I'm telling you, Hannah. That bird had a mind of its own. Bruno opened the front, back, and side doors so the bird could fly out. That bird flew upstairs and downstairs for another ten minutes before she finally decided to fly out the front door. I'm telling you, that bird left when she was good and ready to go and not before. She had a mind of her own."

After laughing with them for another minute, I said, "I'm glad you two can laugh at it and not be upset that you had to stay in your apartments all day because of a harmless little bird," I joked.

Tarrin said, "I still say it was a huge blackbird. I don't care what Kam says. That bird was gigantic."

"We just had to tell you, Hannah. We hoped it would make you laugh because we know how much you like birds," they said in unison.

EVILNESS HAS NO ENDZONE

I really, really tried to make our marriage work, but as Scotty took more and more of the pain pills and started calling his psychic before he made any decisions, things got progressively and indescribably worse. He did such evil, mean, and hateful things that I found it harder and harder to stay in the marriage.

One Saturday, we drove to Johnson Creek shopping mall, about forty-five minutes from Madison. While Scotty and I shopped at different stores, I ran into our neighbors from Madison. The two sisters had taken the bus to the mall, and I invited them to ride back to Madison with Scotty and me. I told them Scotty planned to leave at 6:30 p.m. and said we could meet at the coffee shop at 6:00 p.m.

Scotty had been pleasant on the drive to Johnson Creek, and I wrongly assumed he would be okay with me inviting our neighbors to ride back with us. Even though he and I were enjoying a genteel outing, and he was in a good mood, I forgot how cold-blooded he could be.

He exploded in rage when I told him I had invited Marie and Dorothy to ride home with us. "How can you tell someone to ride with us without asking me? Did you ask me what my plans were? Do you even care? Maybe I don't feel like having guests ride back with me. I don't like you making those decisions without consulting me, Hannah."

"It's no big deal, Scotty. We have room in the car, and you don't have to drive out of your way because they live across the street from us."

"If it's no big deal, just ride the bus back with them!"

I didn't think he was serious about me riding the bus back. "I told them to meet us in the coffee shop at 6:00 p.m."

"Go find them now. I'm ready to leave right now!"

I glanced at my wristwatch. "It's only 4:00 p.m. I told Marie and Dorothy we would meet at 6:00 p.m. You said you wanted to head back at 6:30 p.m. I'm sure they're not in the coffee shop now. I have no idea where they might be."

"Call them on their cell and tell them I'm ready to go now! I'm leaving them if they're not here in ten minutes."

My mouth gaped, and my head shook. "I don't have their cell numbers." My eyes darted toward several stores. "I'll check to see if they're in the coffee shop; if not, I'll search for them in the mall."

He looked at his wristwatch and then at me. "Why are you still standing here?"

"I'll be back as soon as I find them."

As I suspected, they were not in the coffee shop. Scampering through the small mall, I peeped into several stores looking for Green Bay Packers shirts with numbers 4 and 31 written on them. As I came out of Bath and Body Works, I spotted them entering Old Navy. Half jogging and walking to the other side, I shouted, "Marie! Dorothy!"

My hands waved above my head like a flag swaying in the wind. The women halted in front of the door to Old Navy when they spotted me waving. I told them Scotty was ready to leave if they wanted to ride back with us.

The sisters nodded and said, "Yes."

We rushed to the spot where I had left Scotty, and no Scotty was waiting. My face grew hot, and I blinked back tears as embarrassment crawled over me. *I know he didn't leave me here at the mall. That's my car he's driving.* I forced a tight-lipped smile while glancing around the mall. "I'm not sure where he could be. Maybe he went to the bathroom. Let's stay by the exit door, so we won't miss him."

For ten minutes, we waited by the door. One eyebrow lifted, Dorothy asked, her face blushing. "Do you think he left us?"

My head shook. "He couldn't have. He told me to find you. Maybe he went to bring the car closer and is waiting for us outside."

We lugged our shopping bags to the parking lot, and I looked around for my car and Scotty. No Scotty. After wandering around in the parking lot for thirty minutes, I accepted the fact that he had left his wife at the mall. My heart sank deep into my gut, my voice stammered when I spoke, and I couldn't maintain eye contact; I was so embarrassed.

Marie and Dorothy tried to make it less severe, saying we could stay at the mall until it closed and shop until we dropped! But my insides gyrated from embarrassment, and I felt like cow manure. *How could he do that? How could he justify leaving his wife at a mall?*

We ate at Applebee's, shopped till the mall closed, and caught the last bus headed to Madison. When I walked into the house, Scotty shouted from the bedroom, "I waited on you, and after you weren't back, I figured you decided to catch the bus back with your neighbors, and I see you did."

"I caught the bus back because you left me stranded at the mall! We were back and ready to go in less than ten minutes, and you were already gone. That is so heartless, Scotty."

"You should know me by now, Hannah. When I say I'm ready to go, I'm ready to go, and I will leave anyone if they're not ready."

"But I'm your wife, and you're not supposed to leave your wife."

"Says who?"

He had done many cruel things to me, but this hurt me to the core. Instead of talking about my emotions, it didn't do any good anyway; I withdrew from Scotty and stopped talking to him. He was okay with me not conversing because we didn't communicate much anyway. But he wouldn't tolerate it when I moved into the guest bedroom.

While lying in the guest bed, thinking and meditating, my breath decreased, and my pulse slowed to a resting heart rate. Scotty yelled my name. I did not respond, and the next minute, Scotty stood in the doorway.

"Why are you in this bedroom?" He leaned against the door with arms crossed.

"I'm going to sleep in here from now on."

He didn't say another word. He snatched the comforter off of me, threw it on the floor, grabbed the collar of my pajamas, and dragged me back to the main bedroom. "You're my wife, and I will not have my wife sleeping in a different bedroom."

My body trembled, and my pulse throbbed in my neck like a small animal cornered by a lion, unsure if the event would escalate to a physical fight. But I tried to keep my composure and not show fear. The room suffocated me, and beads of sweat formed on my forehead despite the coolness of the spring air. I took relaxed breaths to calm my pounding heart and racing breaths.

I crawled into bed with my back facing him and snuggled under the covers, wondering why he insisted on his wife sleeping with him when we didn't cuddle, caress, touch, talk, or make love.

Scotty's cup overflowed with evilness. While I continued being a faithful, obedient wife, he persisted in doing malicious and hateful deeds. A few weekends after the mall outing, he persuaded me to spend a weekend at Moses's summer cabin in northern Wisconsin. He said, "This will be a weekend of relaxation and no arguments, I promise. We can catch fish, go boating, swim, or you can just relax at the lake."

Still hoping to salvage our marriage, I agreed to go with him. The fire had died, but I expected a few embers could spark another blaze.

Since his fuse was very short and he got angry at the drop of a hat, something I did at the cabin upset him. An incident so trivial I can't even remember what enraged him. Perhaps it was for not cooking when he said he was hungry after we reached the cabin, refusing to go on the lake in the boat with him Friday evening, or staying in bed when he woke me at 5:00 a.m. Saturday morning. Whatever the case, he decided I needed punishment for disrespecting and disobeying him. While I was still asleep Saturday morning, he got up before dawn and locked me in the cabin.

When I awoke, I searched for him and called his name several times. I slid on my slippers, walked to the front door, and couldn't open it. After twisting and pulling on the locked door, I assumed Scotty had inadvertently locked it when he went out. Tingles ran through my body when I checked the back door, and it was also deadbolted. *I know he didn't!* The car was missing, and he was nowhere to be seen when *I* peeped through the windows hoping to spot him on the grounds.

Not wanting to believe he would invite me to an isolated area and then leave me, I figured he'd be back in several minutes and locked the doors to keep anyone from walking in on me while I slept.

My stomach growled. *I might as well eat some breakfast. Maybe Scotty will be back by the time I've finished breakfast. I think I'll make pancakes this morning.*

While making breakfast, the cabin got hot, and sweat dribbled down my face. I went to open the windows, and to my disbelief, they wouldn't open. *What is wrong with that man? It's going to get very hot in here as the day progresses.* Fortunately, Moses had ceiling fans in all the rooms, and I turned them all on to cool the house.

Still no Scotty by the time I finished eating breakfast.

By sundown, I began to worry about Scotty. I didn't fathom at the time that he purposely locked me in the cabin. *I hope nothing has happened to him. Where could he be? I hope he didn't fall into the lake.*

By 9:00 p.m., I considered calling the police. *I should call the police and report a missing person,* I thought. *But what if he's not missing? Then you'll look like a fool,* a voice whispered in my head. *Call his cell.* I had sat all day waiting on him and not thought to try calling him. I guess I expected him to walk through the door at any moment.

"Scotty? Where are you? I was getting worried. I'm locked in this cabin."

"I know."

"You know?"

"That's what I said. I didn't stutter, did I?"

My heart raced so fast I couldn't speak for a moment. "That's ludicrous! Why in heaven would you lock me in the cabin? And where are you? You said this was going to be a relaxing weekend without fighting."

"You've been too sassy lately. You're getting too big for your britches and need to be more respectful to your *daddy*. I do all I can to please and make you happy, and you don't appreciate it. Hopefully, by Sunday evening, you will have thought about your ways and how good you have it. A lot of women would love to be in your shoes. I expect some improvement when I pick you up."

I was too appalled to speak. It wouldn't do any good anyway. Once Scotty made up his mind about something, he stuck with it. He thought people were weak and wishy-washy when they changed their minds.

I decided to make lemonade out of lemon, an omelet out of cracked eggs, and sour cream out of bad milk. It was supposed to be a weekend of rest, and it was definitely more relaxing without Scotty. I decided to turn the weekend into a spiritual retreat for myself. I spent the rest of Saturday and Sunday praying, reading the Bible, meditating, and seeking more of Yahweh's thoughts. Granted, I was locked in the cabin, but I had plenty of food, water, air circulating, and toiletries.

A LIVING NIGHTMARE

Scotty's abuse was progressing from verbal to threatened physical. I tried to blame it on the drugs because I didn't want to admit that I had gotten myself entrapped in another verbally and physically abusive marriage. After the cabin incident, during an argument, he grabbed a bronze statue and threatened to hit me with it if I moved my lips to say another word. My eyes enlarged as I stepped away from him. I felt it was another one of his intimidations, but I couldn't be sure.

I tell you no lie, he got increasingly violent, and I had to pray for protection twenty-four hours a day.

Regrettably, I believed the leopard's spots would change, and the dog would not return to his vomit. I continued to pray for change in us and our marriage.

After existing in a living hell for two years of dating and marriage of almost two years, I softly but confidently told Scotty the marriage was not working. "Both of us are unhappy. You spend more time with your youth group, your lady friends, or talking to your female friends than you do with me. Why are you even staying married? Maybe it would be best to look for another place to stay."

"It's not over until I say it's over! I have invested a lot of money in this house, and you think I will walk away from all my investment?" His face contorted, twisting into the image of a black bear, and his hands slowly bawled into fists as he stood over me.

A rotten egg, musty, and musky odor emanated from him. *What is that disgusting scent?* Scotty always smelled like expensive cologne. I couldn't imagine why this odor was coming from him.

The Holy Spirit warned me to cease talking. I had much to say, but this was not the time. The angry spirit was taking over Scotty's body, and I did not know what he might do if I continued discussing the issue. I wanted to tell him that he had not invested anything in the house because he used his money to buy expensive gifts for his female friends.

He and Moses raked in money from their DME and transportation businesses, but he didn't use any of it to assist me. I have no idea how he spent his pension income from his twenty-five-year military career and his twenty-year civilian employment at a chemical plant.

During one of our bill discussions, he scoffed, "You were paying your bills before you married me, weren't you? I can't understand why you're having problems paying your bills now. You must not be managing your money. Maybe you should talk to a financial planner and pay them to help you develop a budget."

I retorted, "If you still had your place, you would be paying rent and utilities, so what's the problem with helping out with the mortgage and utilities here? You would be paying it someplace anyway."

"Like I said, you were doing fine before you married me. What are you doing with your money now that we're married that you don't have enough to keep your bills paid? You must be giving it to some *young* man. And I won't help you take care of no young hustler."

He had no problems using his money to pay for us to go to expensive restaurants, plays, and concerts but didn't think he had any obligation to assist with household expenses since it wasn't his house. After I refused several times to add his name to the house contract, he contributed little to the household expenses.

He tried convincing me multiple times that having him on the mortgage was in my best interest. "The interest rates are really low now, sweetheart. We should refinance the loan while the rates are low and apply for a home improvement loan. We would have a better chance of getting approval with my income and my name on the application. We could do lots of improvements around here and make this house look like a home."

"I'll think about it, okay?"

"That's right. You'll think about it. Do what you want! It's your house! I don't feel like this is my home – it's *yours*! I told you I don't want anything of yours. I'm trying to help you out. Apparently, you don't trust me enough to add my name to the deed on the house. Why should I be concerned about your mortgage? You refuse to put my name on the contract and think you can put me out anytime you want and make me homeless. I gave up my apartment to move in here and invested a lot in this house. And I don't even feel comfortable here!"

All of the bills and the mortgage were in my name. He refused to add his name to any of the household bills but paid for a phone, satellite, and cable television added in his name. He also had expensive media, music systems, and electronic gadgets installed and had everything AT&T sold added to his phone line. But those were all for his enjoyment.

How deceived he was. How deceived Satan had him. He genuinely thought that he contributed much to the upkeep of my home and would not let me take advantage of him. And I could not convince him differently.

Toward the end of our marriage, my house was in worse shape since I married Scotty than when I was single. He tried aerating the lawn but ended up killing the grass and leaving dirt spots all over the property where green grass should have been sprouting. The landscaping was atrocious, with dead grass patches and weeds in the flower beds. My fence was falling and needed repair. The roof was leaking. One of the water heaters stopped working, and the other didn't heat the water. All of the faucets in the home dripped. The whole house needed paint inside, and the gutters and trim needed painting outside. Additionally, pink disconnection notices for the electricity, gas, and water started arriving in the mailbox. Since I had made partial mortgage payments for several months, the house would be foreclosed if I didn't pay the total amount within thirty days.

I quit one of my three jobs because I expected my husband to assist me. My business was in the growing stage and wasn't bringing in the money that I had projected. Expenses had doubled in the past year. My rent, gas, and electricity bills increased from when I first signed the lease. I contemplated finding another job to keep from losing my home, but I didn't want to do anything until Scotty was out of my life and home.

For the first few months of our marriage, I worked three jobs but quit the school job after he bought expensive gifts for his female friends. Around the same time, the hospital downsized and stopped using me as often, even canceling the already approved hours. The unit census was low, and the full-time and part-time employees received hours before the on-call workers.

THE BREAKING POINT

With my decrease in personal income and Scotty contributing minimally, I prayed in the morning, throughout the day, and at night for God's provision. And I thought I was dealing with Scotty's deviousness, tirades, and exasperating behaviors by attending Bible study, women's ministry, and Sunday services.

One night, while working my third shift at the hospital, I listened in on the Unit Clerk and certified nurse's assistant (CNA) discussing abusive men. The nursing assistant said, "I ain't gonna let no man hit me. I throw whatever I can put my hands on at him."

The Unit Clerk replied, "My gramma told me always to keep a set of cast iron skillets and hit him with one if he abused me."

The ladies laughed loudly. A nurse strolled to them and said, "My mom told me to throw boiling water in his face, and if I really wanted him to pay for hitting me, put some hominy grits in the boiling water and throw that in his face."

They laughed again and gave each other high-five hand slaps.

I pretended to chart nursing notes as I listened. *I'm going to need to get bold like those girls.*

The CNA added, "I'm from Louisiana. My husband knows I sleep with a butcher knife under my pillow."

As I stood, I glanced and smiled at the Unit Clerk. "I'm going to make rounds," I said.

While I checked on my patients, I chuckled at their conversation. After finishing my rounds, I didn't think about it anymore. I finished my charting, closed out charts, and headed home from my graveyard, 11 p.m. to 7 a.m. shift. On my way home, I stopped by the grocers and picked up laundry detergent, fruit, juice, and breakfast food.

Scotty peered through the blinds as I pulled into the driveway. I threw my purse and nurse's bag over my shoulders and shuffled to the door with shopping bags in each hand.

When I stepped on the porch, Scotty snatched the door open. I smiled and dropped the bags on the porch, thinking he was coming to assist me.

Because I was an hour late getting home from work, Scotty was vehement. "It's almost 9 a.m., and you're strolling in the house like it's 7:30 a.m. You expect me to believe you worked all night and then went grocery shopping. I'm no idiot, woman. You claim you're so tired when you work the third shift job that you don't have the energy to do anything but sleep. So where have you been all night? You come in here with grocery bags. I'm not falling for that trick. I invented it." He wiped saliva spooling at the corner of his mouth and continued his rant. "I called the hospital, and they said you weren't on duty. They wouldn't tell me whether you worked last night or not. I'm getting sick of ...."

"Are you going to help me bring the bags in?"

He stared, scowling and without blinking as he blocked the doorway.

"Excuse me. I want to go in the house."

He glared and blocked the entranceway, his nostrils flaring, his jaws clenched, and his eyes bulging.

I picked up the bags, looked him in the eyes, and squeezed past him, pushing his back to the door.

Scotty limped to the island in the kitchen, where I had placed the bags, holding onto the furniture because he didn't bring his cane. He took items out of bags, slamming them onto the countertop. "You bought a lot of breakfast food. I only want three slices of bacon, two poached eggs, toast, and coffee."

"I bought this to cook breakfast tomorrow since I don't have to work tomorrow night."

"I want breakfast this morning. I may not want breakfast tomorrow morning."

"You know how to cook, Scotty. I have not slept for nearly twenty-four hours. I couldn't sleep before work last night. I will drop from sleep deprivation if I don't lie down."

"You couldn't have been that tired. You *supposedly* spent an hour in the store this morning."

Heading toward the bedroom, I turned my back to him. He grabbed the collar of my top and pulled my face backward until his nose almost touched mine. He glared into my pupils, hyper-extending my neck. "Don't turn your back to me when I'm talking to you. I want my breakfast in the next hour." He released my collar and limped to the bedroom.

For several seconds, time froze as I stood paralyzed, reflecting on what had just happened. Scotty shouted obscenities from the bedroom.

An exasperated and loud sigh dropped from my mouth. *I don't feel like making breakfast, especially now that Scotty harassed me and demanded that I cook.* My jaws clenched as I kicked the table. *But if*

I don't, he won't let me sleep and will continue to nag and harass me. Maybe by the time breakfast is ready, he will have calmed down and be more rational.

Choosing not to fight, I prepared breakfast, sat it at the table, and informed Scotty that his breakfast was on the table. The pulse in my neck throbbed when he hobbled from the back to the kitchen table.

Scotty didn't apologize, say thank you for cooking breakfast, or acknowledge that I was standing in the room. He sat, leaned his cane against the wall, and started eating.

I started boiling water and pulled the grits out of the cabinet.

Scotty complained that the eggs were not poached and started his tirade of putting me down and humiliating me.

I poured the grits into the boiling water. The hominy started bubbling in the pot. I slowly slid my hands into oven mitts.

Scotty's voice sounded louder and louder and louder in my head. The exact words circled in my head: *"You can't do anything right, you can't do anything right, you can't do anything right."*

It was as if another person grabbed the boiling grits by the handles and walked towards Scotty with the bubbling grits.

Scotty sipped his coffee, blind to what was happening behind him.

The bubbling grits lifted to my chest level, and I took another step toward him. Scotty didn't discern the stiffening quietness in the room or hear me approaching. The pot tilted in his direction, but before the boiling hominy left the pan to shampoo Scotty, a voice whispered, *"It's not worth it, Hannah. He's not worth it. Please don't do it. What would it solve? You'd be stooping to his level and be just as evil and ungodly as he is. There is a better way – walk in it."*

Scriptures from my Bible study class, women's Bible group, and our pastors' sermons flooded my mind while I stood with the bubbling kettle of grits wobbling over Scotty's head. "Thank you, Holy Spirit," I whispered as I placed the hot pan back on the stove.

"What did you say?" Scotty asked, snarling.

"I'm going to bed."

After showering and lying in bed, I asked God what had happened in the kitchen. "How did I allow myself to get filled with so much evil and hate that I was willing to pour hot grits on Scotty? Has Scotty's spirits jumped on me?"

"You allowed the spirits of hurt, anger, resentment, and revenge to set up camp in your temple," a voice whispered. "The words from the women at work fueled the fire and permitted the evil spirits to operate.

DRIVE OUT A SCOFFER

Being married to Scotty was exceedingly and abundantly more unbearable than I ever could have imagined. But I was determined to be a sanctified, submissive, obedient wife, even if it killed me. And it almost did.

The following Wednesday night, the pastor taught about strife and bitterness during Bible study. He had us turn to Proverbs 22, verse 10 (RSV),

> *"Drive out a scoffer, and strife will go out, and quarreling and abuse will cease."*

The scripture seemed to yell at me – *drive out a scoffer, and strife will go out, and quarreling and abuse will cease. Are you speaking to me, Holy Spirit?"*

Since we married, Scotty and I had nothing but strife, quarreling, and abuse. I had to decide whether to stay in an abusive, strife-filled, and quarrelsome marriage or drive the scoffer out. Dr. Joyce had talked about a scoffer in one of our sessions, and Aunt Lucy talked about a scoffer during our last conversation. The word scoffer was mentioned thrice in one week, and I paid attention. Perhaps the Holy Spirit was trying to tell me something.

It would take months of more abuse before I understood that emotional adultery and verbal, emotional, and sexual abuse (withholding sex), and hate, bitterness, strife, condemnations, ridicule, and accusations were enough for me to divorce Scotty without guilt.

The Bible clearly stated that man and wife were to come together sexually:

> *"The husband must give the wife what is due to her, and equally, the wife must give the husband his due. The wife cannot claim her body as her own; it is her husband's. Equally, the husband cannot claim his body as his own; it is his wife's. Do not deny yourselves to one another, except when you agree to devote yourselves to prayer for a time, and to come together again afterwards; otherwise, through lack of self-control, you may be tempted by Satan"* I Corinthians 7:3-5 (REV).

After reading this scripture, I felt confident I would not be out of the will of God by divorcing Scotty. His withholding sex was a form of abuse.

I believe Scotty hoped I would commit adultery; then, in his mind, he would have something to accuse me of and possibly kill me for. In my heart, I don't think Scotty would have given killing me a second thought if he had caught me committing adultery. Scotty often said I was a young woman and had sexual desires. But he didn't do anything as my husband to fulfill those desires.

Honestly, I'm unsure if I remained a faithful and virtuous wife due to self-control, fear of God, or fear of Scotty. I hope it was fear of God and loving Him more than sex and pleasing my flesh.

The revelation the Holy Spirit gave me about our marriage being a *Wormwood marriage* came to mind. We had been married exactly one-third of a year when the scales fell entirely off of my eyes. It took several more months before I ended the union. People didn't die as the scripture said, but many things died in me during the time with Scotty Brian.

Waters didn't turn bitter, but my marriage became very sour from the fourth month and grew more pungent until I gained the courage to end it. Our marriage had been built on sand and not on the *Rock,* as stated in Matthew 7:24-27 (REV).

> *"So whoever hears these words of mine and acts on them is like a man who had the sense to build his house on rock. The rain came down, the floods rose, the winds blew and beat upon that house; but it did not fall, because its foundations were on rock. And whoever hears these words of mine and does not act on them is like a man who was foolish enough to build his house on sand. The rain came down, the floods rose, the winds blew and battered against that house; and it fell with a great wrath."*

When problems arose, Scotty's lies multiplied. The rains descended, and the floods came. The winds blew and beat upon our marriage with financial, relational, domestic, and emotional problems. Our union could not stand. The marital bond could not withstand the tornados, thunderstorms, and hurricanes that appeared in the form of abuse, mayhem, dishonor, and disrespect. There was no restoration after the crash.

First Corinthians, chapter thirteen illuminated and had more significance. After our fourth month of marriage, when reading my journal notes, my spiritual eyesight perfected; I discerned that Scotty did not love me with the thirteenth chapter of Corinthians love. But I thought if I worked harder at demonstrating this kind of love, Scotty would reciprocate.

Clinging onto a dead Wormwood Marriage, I went to work trying to display true love to my husband.

Though I speak with the tongues of men and of angels, but have not love, I have become sounding brass or a clanging cymbal. And though I have the gift of prophecy, and understand all mysteries and all knowledge, and though I have all faith; so that I could remove mountains, but have not love, I am nothing. And though I bestow all my goods to feed the poor, and though I give my body to be burned, but have not love, it profits me nothing. 'Love suffers long and is kind; love does not envy; love does not parade itself, is not puffed up; does not behave rudely, does not seek its own, is not provoked, thinks no evil; does not rejoice in iniquity, but rejoices in the truth; bears all things, believes all things, hopes all things, endures all things. Love never fails. But whether there are prophecies, they will fail; whether there are tongues, they will cease; whether there

<blockquote>
is knowledge, it will vanish away. ....And now abideth faith, hope, love, these three; but the greatest of these is love I Corinthians 13: 1-8, 13 (RSV).
</blockquote>

Working harder to demonstrate the 13th chapter of Corinthians' love did not affect Scotty whatsoever. He actually seemed to become more hateful and bitter. When we dated, he acted concerned about my safety, standing on the porch until I was in my car and had driven a block down the street. After we married, he would be asleep when I went to work at 11:00 p.m.

I also thought he wanted his new bride with him at night instead of working all night at a job. Instead of telling me to quit, he encouraged me to request more hours at the hospital. I began to think I had married a gigolo and that he expected his wife to work three jobs, pay all of the bills, and he could spend his money in any way he desired.

Before we married, Scotty said he didn't think ladies should mop floors, and his wife would not be mopping floors. Well, I cleaned floors weekly without any assistance from him. He didn't mop one floor, wash one dish, dust one piece of furniture, or clean one toilet after we married. Unless he was trying to manipulate me after I demonstrated I was agitated. He wouldn't lift one finger to help me with the house cleaning but always found fault with how the house looked after my cleaning.

Maybe it was his military background, but he did the white glove test after I cleaned. He always found a spot on the table not dusted, crust left on the dishes, kitchen appliances not scrubbed spotless, and tile in the bathroom filthy.

One Saturday, he took out a toothbrush, scrubbed two horizontal sheets of the beige bedroom blinds, and then handed me the toothbrush. "These blinds are filthy and need to be scrubbed down, " he said.

While I stared with my arms folded across my chest, he pointed to the kitchen and said, "The kitchen blinds need washing too, and you may as well clean the tile in the bathrooms and get the scum out."

With one raised eyebrow and a slightly tucked chin, I replied, "Okay," strutted to the living room, and started watching a Hallmark movie.

Another Saturday, while changing bed linen, he yelled when he spotted dirty linen on the floor. "Don't put my pillows on the floor, you nasty wench!"

"The pillowcases are going in the wash anyway. What difference does it make?"

"I don't want my pillows on the floor even if the pillowcases go in the wash."

He found fault with everything I did. It took a while, but I learned he was trying to kill my spirit and steal my self-esteem by making me think I couldn't do anything right.

"Drive out a scoffer? Um?" I meditated on Proverbs 22, verse 10.

BOSTON MATHESON

S cotty tried to entice BM to Madison for nearly a year and got increasingly more irritated when Boston changed his plans at the last minute. He thought Boston had been in Madison numerous times since our meeting with him in Chicago. Scotty decided it was time to have another face-to-face with BM. He called Boston and told him we would be in Chicago and would look him up once we arrived. We met him at his trucking office since he wanted to give Scotty a tour of his operation.

When we pulled in front of the building, a good-looking man who looked taller than 6 feet and at least 300 pounds stood outside. His size reminded me of 'The Refrigerator,' a defensive tackle for the Chicago Bears in the eighties. He sported a beautiful olive green and black sweater with black slacks. He swaggered to our car, opened the door for me, smiled, and said, "Good morning, madam." He dashed to the other side and opened the door for Scotty with the same greeting, "Good morning, Sir. How was your drive from Madison?"

"Fine. And who are you?" Scotty retorted.

"I'm your little fairy godfather, taking you to Wonderland." He let out a deep belly laugh, looked at Scotty, and noticed he was scowling and non-smiling. He replied, "I'm just joking, man. I work for Mr. Matheson." He opened one of the double glass doors and escorted us into an elegantly designed building.

"This is a gorgeous building. I didn't expect a trucking business to have such glamorous decor. I said, glancing around. "And such beautiful artwork."

"Mr. Matheson has good taste and thinks it doesn't have to look like a trucking business in the office areas. It works for me because I can charm the women when I bring them here. They are always so impressed." He smiled and winked at me.

My shoulders jerked backward, and my brows arched. *Is this young whippersnapper flirting with me?*

We strolled to an elevator and went up several floors before he pushed floor thirteen. "This is the end of the road for you!" The door opened, and blackness caused me to squint until my pupils enlarged. Multiple gigantic boxes stacked on each other filled the space in the dark warehouse.

Scotty and I didn't move. We just stared at the huge man who never told us his name. While I studied our escort, his hair made me think of King David's son, Absalom. His head was full of thick locks, with the top half pulled back in a ponytail and the bottom half flowing down his back.

Our chaperone burst with his deep belly laugh. "I just like to have fun." His eyes narrowed as he gazed at Scotty. "Get a sense of humor, man. Laugh more! Enjoy life! Don't take everything so seriously." He pressed floor twenty and continued chuckling until the doors slid open.

We stepped off at floor twenty, and he escorted us to BM's luxurious office.

Boston strode to us, kissed me on the cheek, and gave Scotty a shoulder hug. "It's good to see you again, Mr. Scotty and Miss Hannah. I apologize that I haven't been able to make it to Madison. Every time I planned to visit you, something went wrong in the business, and I had to cancel. I'm glad you were able to come here this weekend. Did Don Juan scare you with some of his antics?"

"That's his name, Don Juan? He's a character, that's for sure. Scare me? I doubt it." Scotty said grandiloquently, pushing his chest out.

When I glanced in his direction, Don Juan smiled at me. His eyes showed kindness and gentleness, something I didn't read in Scotty's or BM's eyes. Instead, hardness, coldness, and callousness sparked from their pupils. Don Juan reminded me of a giant teddy bear waiting for a cuddle. I sensed he was tough and could be mean if needed, but I also viewed his light, kind, and fun side.

While touring the plant, we spotted Don Juan laughing, dancing, and clowning around in one of the rooms with other employees. He, like BM, had a beautiful smile and straight, white teeth. To be such a large man, he was light on his feet. I couldn't help but smile while I studied him; he seemed to enjoy life.

I commented, "Don seems like a likable person. He sure likes to have fun."

"He likes to be called *Don Juan,*" BM replied. "He is a likable person, and the women are crazy about him. He understands how to treat a lady. Most of the men in the building ask him for advice when they're having problems with their women. He says he is a connoisseur of women. Don Juan is cool." His head nodded.

"He's a handsome man too, big but strikingly handsome." Scotty glanced sideways at me, and I quickly added, "Handsome for much younger women. I'm old enough to be his mother. And I'm an old married lady."

With many cell phone interruptions and apologies from BM, we finished the tour.

"What sort of things do you ship?" I asked, curious about the giant boxes on the thirteenth floor.

"Mostly medical supplies," Boston said. "We have partnerships with several small transportation businesses around the country. Most of our routes go to small towns where the larger trucking companies don't want to go."

"Those sound like good relationships," I said.

BM flashed his crowning smile, "We have a few contracts with bigger corporations as their primary transporter also."

Scotty said nothing, glaring with a tight-lipped, fake smile.

I tapped Boston's shoulder. "I'm proud of you, young man, stepping out to start your own business."

BM smiled as we headed back to his office suite.

BM, Don Juan, and the three dapperly dressed men with him the first time we called on him took us to a fancy Italian restaurant in Indiana. The women swarmed around Don Juan and flirted with Boston but did not invade his space. Don Juan joked with the ladies, bought roses from a flower peddler, and gave each lady a rose. He promised to connect with them later in the evening. While Don Juan flirted, one eye stayed in BM's direction, the other scanning the room for unusual activity. He demonstrated responsibility for his job duties and did not slack in protecting BM.

Scotty scolded Boston for not visiting Madison as promised, almost making him swear he would come to Thanksgiving dinner. BM was getting more comfortable with Scotty and didn't seem as uptight and mistrusting as in our prior interactions. After dinner, BM had one of his men take us back to our car, saying he had a meeting at the restaurant later.

PLAYER GETS PLAYED

O n the drive home, Scotty rambled, "That's a slick front BM uses to deliver his drugs." His head nodded. "He transports his products as medical supplies around the country as the front for his drug empire." His right jaw twitched. "He even has legitimate trucking conglomerates distributing his products."

Against my better judgment, I said, "You don't know that, Scotty. Perhaps his business is legit."

Scotty lowered his head to his right shoulder, peered at me over his eyeglasses, and said, "Hum. If his business is legit, I'm a billionaire."

The next day, Scotty started researching Boston Matheson's trucking business and searched Madison for the king of the Madison drug lords. Scotty learned that Chicagoland residents and businesspeople respected BM. He donated large sums to politicians, influential ministers, and needy non-profit organizations. Most people in Chicago categorized Boston as a community advocate.

Scotty discovered the king of the south side Madison drug lord's leader was a former cop called DC, for death cop. The nickname – Death Cop stuck when rumors spread that he killed all witnesses scheduled to testify against him for being associated with a gang as a police officer. Stories floated that DC took bribes, stole drug cartel money, was addicted to cocaine, and left no witnesses if pulled over by him. Thus the name – Death Cop.

Scotty could charm a cobra and was shrewd at getting the information he wanted. People either loved him or hated him. He treated the ones he didn't need or didn't care about with scorn, disgust and disrespect, and a pompous attitude. Those were the ones that hated him. He charmed and smooth-talked others and went out of his way to assist if he required them for information or favors. Those were the ones who thought he was the greatest thing since cell phones and thought he was honest, considerate, and caring. Those were the ones who loved him.

Scotty somehow got the legal name for DC. His legal name was David Carlyle, but no one knew that but the Madison police department. On the streets, he was known only as DC.

Scotty convinced one of DC's underlings to set up a meeting with him to discuss a business proposition. Not being privy to this discussion, I eavesdropped while he talked on the phone to his contact. "Why can't I talk directly to the man? I don't like going through a go-between because information gets misconstrued. Pause.

What do you mean he *don't* talk on the phone? He does all of his business face-to-face. Well, set up a meeting for me to meet him face to face. Pause again. He won't meet with me. How in hades do you know if you haven't asked him? I have some information I'm sure he will be interested in hearing, and I'm not telling anyone but him. Another pause. You do that. Yeah, call me back at this number when you hear from him."

The contact didn't call back that night, and Scotty roared like a lion. At some point, however, Scotty arranged a meeting. A few nights later,

Scotty dressed and hid the switchblade above the pins in his hip so it wouldn't buzz if they scanned him. He picked up Mr. Benny but then decided against taking the pistol.

An hour later, he limped into the house in a cheerful mood, impressed with what he thought he had accomplished. He bragged as he drank root beer and snacked on chips. "Death Cop knows Boston Matheson is trying to take over his south side territory and will handle his business. They don't call him Death Cop for nothing. He's a former cop, knows how to handle a weapon, and still has loyal friends on the police force. I have no doubt he will take care of BM for me. Well, for himself, but he will also be doing me a favor."

Acting uninterested, I washed dishes with my back to him, knowing he would give more information if I didn't ask questions.

"Don't you want to know how I did this?"

"I'm not sure what you're talking about. I didn't know you knew this DC guy, and what makes you think he knows Boston wants his territory."

"You are such a dumb lady. I thought you were smart when I married you, but I was dead wrong. How do you think I know? I met with DC and told him. I told him I was telling him because I didn't want gang wars in my neighborhood. So if he and BM could work it out between them, maybe they could keep the violence to a minimum.

But DC takes no hostages! And he won't be talking, probably shooting. Ha ha ha."

"I thought you had begun to really like Boston. I think he genuinely likes you."

"That's why I say you're one dumb lady, Hannah. That was the plan all the time, to convince BM to think of me as a daddy, to trust me, and bang, I've gotten revenge for Charlessa's death. It was all his fault. If she hadn't been involved with him, she would still be alive instead of me having to....."

"Instead of you having to what?" I think he was about to tell me about him calling her from the dead.

"Nothing. Forget it. We're talking about Boston Matheson paying for his crime."

I turned to face Scotty.

"I told DC that BM would be at our house for Thanksgiving and laid out my plan. I'll take BM on a tour of the University since he claims he's never been to Madison." Scotty's face disappeared in a grin. "DC's gang is going to carjack me, throw me out, and kidnap BM."

My hands went to my hips, and I sighed. Scotty had it all mapped out.

BM didn't come for Thanksgiving dinner, and Scotty was furious because it ruined his credibility with DC. He thought he had Boston eating out of his hands. Scotty paced the floor, cursing when he couldn't reach Boston.

Trying to reassure himself, Scotty mumbled, "Maybe he's already dead. Maybe DC went to Chicago or trapped BM when he was here on drug business."

His face flushed, and his eyes squinted when he couldn't contact DC's underling, his go-between person, nor reach BM. It was as if both men had disappeared off the face of the earth.

Scotty hadn't heard from BM or DC for several weeks, but he didn't seem worried that they might have discovered he was using both. If anything, he was angry and agitated that Boston had not gotten back to him.

As Scotty tried to reach DC's gofer one day, I asked, "What if DC or his go-between guy told BM what you did? What do you think he would do?"

"DC hates BM, and I don't think he told him. And that flunky is a punk and a dummy; he didn't tell anyone anything. BM and DC are both locked away or hiding somewhere."

Scotty glanced sideways at me. "At least I learned something from DC's gofer. That punk thinks BM is a god." He stopped, expecting me to ask questions.

"I would think they'd be too scared to say anything," I said.

Scotty pressed his lips together and shook his head.

"You've got to talk their language. The little peon said BM is smart and cunning enough to transport his drugs in his delivery trucks without anyone becoming suspicious. He said the drugs are hidden behind secret walls and removed before reaching the delivery sites, leaving only the medical supplies in the trucks."

"It sounds like he works for BM instead of DC."

Scotty rolled his eyes. "They all work together, but everyone wants a bigger piece of the pie."

It was not until the beginning of the year that Boston telephoned. He called and told Scotty he was expanding his business internationally and had been out of the country. We had no way of knowing whether he was telling the truth. But what difference did it make? Whether he was locked away or out of the country, he was back, and Scotty was still fixated on killing him.

Scotty smiled into the receiver, put the phone on speaker, and set the phone on the table. "That invitation for dinner is open whenever you want to come up here, BM. I'm beginning to think you don't think my house is good enough for you."

"I'm a busy person, old man, and I don't have time to sip tea and do nothing like you do. Have I ever disrespected you? Have I done or said anything that would make you say something like that to me? I'm hurt by that statement, old man. Truthfully. Anyway, I will see you when I see you. When I decide it's time to come to Madison, I will be there." He sighed into the phone. "But I wasn't playing you when I promised to come Thanksgiving. I had all intentions of coming, but things got out of hand, and I couldn't leave."

Scotty inhaled. "You have treated me like a dad since we hung out in Chicago, so I'm sorry if my statement came out the wrong way."

"Apology accepted," Boston said. "I received your calls and wanted to get back to you to let you know I wasn't dead. But circumstances prevented it. Peace."

"Why would I think you were....?" The line went dead.

"What? He hung up on me. I wasn't through talking. I wonder what Charlessa saw in him. He is an arrogant prick!" He slammed the phone down in the charger.

I could see what she saw in him. Boston was handsome, charming, charismatic, intelligent, a successful businessman, wealthy, and had the most beautiful, whitest, straight teeth I had ever seen.

HOTEL STRANGER

Our marriage was dying like a fish out of water. The nefariousness and bitterness grew like a Mahi Mahi. In my spirit, I sensed our union was waiting for the funeral. But I kept hoping for a miracle, not wanting to be a failure in a second marriage. Friends and family stayed in their marriages and worked through problems; why couldn't Scotty and I do the same?

I prayed that Scotty would have a Damascus Road experience and come home a changed man. Scotty's uncontrollable temper almost got us killed several times. Yet, I prayed for restoring our relationship instead of discerning Yahweh's voice.

On every trip I took with him, chaos and altercations followed. Scotty inevitably found someone with whom to start an argument. If they disagreed with his position, he debated for hours and sometimes threatened physical assault.

Scotty never worried about brawls. I was nearly frightened to death, not knowing if Scotty or the other fellow might draw a switchblade or pistol. My pulse rate is increasing now as I recall an incident where my heart was in my throat. In spring, we drove to East St. Louis to attend a wedding. After going down several dead-end streets, Scotty finally pulled into a service station and asked for directions to the Holiday Inn hotel.

After leaving the service station, Scotty followed the directions given by the attendant. We approached the end of the street, which seemed to be another dead-end, and then spotted a dilapidated, run-down, dingy-looking building with a sign on the side, *oliday Inn*. The H for Holiday was missing, faded away, or buried somewhere on the pavement.

"Why are we stopping here?" I asked. "Are we lost, and you're asking for directions?"

Scotty didn't answer. He turned the ignition off and started rambling through his wallet.

"This is not where we're staying?" I said in a high-pitched tone, my eyes wide. "I thought your cousin said it was an old Holiday Inn. This dump doesn't look like any Holiday Inn I've seen, not even one of the first ones built."

"Stop complaining! We have a place to stay, don't we? At least you're not sleeping on the street like that man over there."

My eyes darted to a homeless male slumped near the side of the building. "The service station man must have given you the wrong directions."

Scotty didn't look at me while he searched through his charge cards. "We may as well stay here tonight, go to the wedding tomorrow, and head back to Madison after the reception."

"This place doesn't look safe." My eyes darted left and right and stopped at the entrance to the building. "Didn't you notice all the homes boarded up and graffiti signs on buildings open for business?"

"No, I didn't."

I pointed upward. "The streetlights are all busted." My head and voice shook. "This parking lot is probably pitch-black when the sun goes down."

"I'm tired of your complaining, Hannah." He gazed at me over his spectacles.

I surveyed the area again while Scotty pulled out charge cards and slid them into his shirt pocket. With only a tiny bit of sun coming from the back of the building, blackness and gloominess covered the front, although it was only 3:00 p.m. A slow, deep sigh crept from my mouth. "Look at that graffiti, Scotty." I pointed to a corner of the hotel. "Those are gang signs."

Scotty's head shook. "That is graffiti. Some punk tagged the building. No big deal." He unhooked his seat belt.

"There is a difference between tagging and gang members' graffiti. That drawing looks like a black Star of David." My voice strengthened. "Taggers usually draw something artistic." I squinted to study the sign. "I don't see anything that looks like a signature, and graffiti taggers sign their work." I added before he could object, "When I took a home-owner's class, they discussed the difference between graffiti tagging and gang signs. Gang members do it to mark off their turf. I think this is a gang area."

Scotty stared at me as if I'd lost my mind. "All we're going to do is sleep in the room. We'll be at the wedding and the reception most of tomorrow and heading home."

"My stomach is jittery. I don't want to stay here. I'll feel safer in a more reputable hotel like the Radisson." I stared at the people entering and exiting the front door. "Or even a newer Holiday Inn."

"You will be with me. You don't have to worry. If anyone messes with me, they are going to regret it."

I was positive the hotel was smack in the middle of gang and drug territory. And controlled by gang members. When I glanced at the slumped man again, I wasn't sure if he was asleep, intoxicated, or dead.

We checked into the hotel, got our room keys, and drove to the side closest to our room. A man in dirty clothes and no teeth held the door open and shouted as if talking to another person. I glanced around and didn't notice anyone but assumed he was yelling for someone down the corridor. We strolled past him, said hello, and headed down the hallway to find the elevator. The man didn't respond to our salutations but looked both of us from head to toe as we passed and shouted for someone to hurry up. I still didn't spot anyone else in the hallway, but the man continued shouting while holding the door open.

We settled in the room, unpacked our clothes for the wedding, and headed to find a Denny's or Perkins restaurant. Men of different ethnicities walked the corridors, hobbled up and down the stairs, and came in and left the hotel as we made our way down the stairs to the exit doors since the elevator was not working.

I thought it strange that we didn't see other women. "I think this is a hotel for transient men, Scotty. Haven't you noticed that there aren't any other women here?"

"There are other women here. Just because you don't see them walking the corridor doesn't mean none are here. There are men, women, and children at this hotel."

I watched all the entrances as we walked to our car and drove around the hotel to the main street. As I surveyed, I didn't spot another female or child. I was positive I was the only woman, and no other women or children were in that hotel.

Unable to find a Denny's or Perkins, we ate at a delicious neighborhood restaurant. As we drove over broken and cracked concrete, maneuvering our way back to the establishment, I looked for signs of another woman or child entering the hotel or coming out. Only more men with missing teeth, uncombed hair, and dirty clothes crossed my view. *This doesn't feel right. I should have seen at least one more female.*

It wouldn't be good to tell Scotty again I was uncomfortable, but I said it nonetheless. "I'm not comfortable staying here. I'm 99% positive this is a building for transient men. I have not seen another female or child for the four hours we've been here. I don't understand why the guy at the desk didn't say something when he saw me with you."

"Stop panicking, Hannah! Other women are staying here. If not, it's no big deal. Nobody will mess with you as long as you're with me. I always keep my 22, Mr. Benny."

When we stepped out of the car and headed for the door, the same feral-looking, unshaven man was holding the door open. The temperature had dropped from the spring 50s to the winter 30s, and Scotty told him to close the door. "You were shouting and holding that darn door four hours ago. If they're not here by now, they're not coming."

The man ignored Scotty and shouted even louder.

That stirred demonic spirits in Scotty, and he snatched the door out of the man's hand and slammed it shut. "Shut the darn door and leave it shut! It's cold in this place." They glared at each other for several seconds, and then the man backed away from Scotty. Scotty glared until the shouter walked down the hallway in the opposite direction.

While Scotty was unlocking the door to our room, the shouter wrapped something around Scotty's neck from behind. The man had sneaked to our floor and had a stocking encircling Scotty's neck, pulling him backward. Scotty punched the man's stomach and tried to swing his cane back to hit him on the knee or shin bone.

I pulled on the man's arms, trying to pull him off Scotty, but he was much stronger than he looked. Scotty fought as best he could, but his punches were not contacting and, therefore, did not make an impact. The perpetrator kicked the cane out of Scotty's hand.

What should I do? Nobody in this hotel would help if I screamed, and I'm sure the man at the front desk didn't care. I've got to do something before he gets Scotty down. Having seen women jump on attackers' backs in movies, I jumped on the man's back and tried choking him with both hands. He released Scotty to knock me off. I held tight, locking my legs around his small frame, squeezing as hard as possible. Scotty caught his breath, reached in his pocket, and pulled out Mr. Benny as the man threw me to the floor.

The assailant turned to finish his attack on Scotty and looked into the face of a 22-caliber pistol. He lunged toward Scotty as if he didn't think the little gun would hurt him.

"NO!" I screamed loud and shrill. My roar startled the attacker, and he stopped in his tracks. "Don't shoot him, Scotty. Can't you tell that something is wrong with him?"

The man turned and walked away as if he had just wrestled with his best friend.

ROAD RAGE

The following weekend, I went with Scotty and Moses to Michigan for a funeral. That trip almost gave me stress incontinence. On our way home, midway through our trip, Scotty played cat and mouse with a semi-truck driver. I awoke from dozing in the back when I heard the guy's hee-hawing. When I opened my eyes to find out what was so funny, Moses looked back, laughed, and pointed at a semi-truck. "What's going on? What's so funny?" I asked.

"Nothing. Go back to sleep," Scotty yelled.

I sat up as the semi-truck passed on the left side. The driver blew his horn, and the guys cackled again. When the truck pulled in front of us, Scotty switched into the left lane and passed the semi, pointing with his fingers and laughing. Scotty hit back into the right lane, and the semi-truck passed on the left. They did this switch-and-pass game for a couple of miles until Scotty threw up his middle finger as he passed.

The men thought the game was amusing. I didn't think so. I was getting more anxious by the minute. I didn't like Scotty and the semi-truck changing lanes so fast and close to each other with so many construction barriers. It was an accident waiting to happen if either driver lost control of their vehicle.

Scotty switched from the left back to the right lane and behind another 18-wheeler. A semi-truck to the left slowed.

Scotty sped to change back to the left lane. Red brake lights beamed from the semi-trailer ahead in the right lane, and the driver straddled both lanes so Scotty couldn't pass. Scotty swerved back into the right lane, and the 18-wheeler pulled back into the right lane. They played this game for another mile, one semi-truck to the left and one in the front. Scotty tried out-maneuvering the truck drivers to pass them, but he was unsuccessful.

I swallowed to lubricate my dry mouth, twisting my wedding ring while sitting on the edge of the back seat, watching the two semi-trailers. After another thirty minutes, Scotty attempted to pass, and the truck drivers let him. My hands covered my heart as I exhaled. The game was over, I thought.

Scotty turned into the left lane, grinning because he thought he had outwitted the truck drivers. The semi behind Scotty drove so close to Scotty's rear bumper that I thought we were getting rear-ended. Scotty sped up to pass the 18-wheeler in the right lane, and it picked up speed. A third semi-truck switched from the right lane to the left in front of Scotty. He was hemmed in by semi-trucks in front, back, and to the right. He couldn't slow down because the truck in the back was on his bumper, he couldn't speed up because the truck in front hit his brakes when Scotty accelerated, and he couldn't switch to the right lane. After all, he didn't have enough space in front of the semi.

The truck drivers toyed with Scotty for another hour, and I guess the one who started the game with Scotty radioed his buddies and told them to let us pass. The semi in front sped up, and the one in the right lane slowed down.

Scotty swerved to the right lane and sped past the 18-wheeler that had blocked him in the front, grinning and holding his middle finger up.

It didn't seem to faze Scotty, but I was scared waterless. He exited at the next exit, and the truck drivers blew their horns as they passed. I admit that I was terrified. I wondered what was going through the truck drivers' heads. I wasn't sure if it was a game or for real. Having watched a movie about a psycho truck driver a few weeks earlier, I had flashes of 18-wheelers flattening us into a small aluminum pancake.

Having passed Chicago's loop, we paid the last toll fee and headed toward Madison. Near Kenosha, Wisconsin, a bright red sports car entered the expressway without yielding to freeway traffic. He dashed onto the freeway inches before us, making Scotty mash his brakes and swerve slightly.

Scotty cursed, calling the traffic breaker every obscene name he could muster, and shook his fist at the driver. He blasted his horn. I tried to calm him down. "Let's pray for him. We don't know why he's in a hurry. Maybe he's rushing to the hospital or is late for work."

"I don't give a darn! He should have left earlier if he was running late. That doesn't give him a reason to cut me off and make me almost have an accident! That's why I always leave in plenty of time, so I'm not rushing and don't have to cut people off." He pressed the accelerator and the car shot forward, trying to catch the bright red car that cut him off. His speed increased to seventy, eighty, and then ninety miles per hour as I monitored the speedometer. "Slow down, Scotty! You're driving too fast and could lose control."

His brother snored in the seat next to him.

Scotty switched from the right to the center lane and passed several vehicles until he spotted the bright red car, now cruising at about fifty-five miles per hour in the right lane. Scotty slowed down, wheeled into the right lane behind the scarlet automobile, and drove his front bumper into the red car's rear bumper.

"Stop it, Scotty! This chase is not funny and could become dangerous."

When the vehicle increased speed and moved into the center lane, I read the Camaro's name at the back. Scotty sped up and changed into the center lane on the tail of the Camaro. They passed several vehicles, and the Apple Red Camaro swerved into the left lane with Scotty right behind him. I tried to talk some sense into Scotty but to no avail. And then I silently started praying for God to keep us safe and asked Jehovah to make the angry, demonic spirits leave Scotty.

The chase continued with both cars changing lanes several times, moving from left to center, back to the left, and then the red car snaked from the left to the right side. Scotty was about one car length behind him. He crossed from the left to the center and into the right lane, still driving as recklessly as the bright red car. The Camaro swerved into the middle lane, then back into the right lane, drove several yards, and his brake lights went on.

"He hit his brakes!" I shouted.

Moses jumped up and asked what was happening, shaking his head and yawning.

Scotty slammed his brakes and jerked to the center lane.

Scotty chuckled. "Just playing a game with a sports car instead of a semi-truck." Scotty switched to the right lane. I thanked God the traffic was not heavy, and the other motorists slowed down when they realized the dangerous game the two cars were playing. The red Camaro sped up again, driving at least one hundred or more miles per hour. Scotty sped after the scarlet car. We spotted brake lights again, and the Camaro exited at Highway 50.

As Scotty exited the Highway 50 exit, still pursuing the Apple Red car, Moses yawned, slid down into the passenger seat, and laid his head against the door.

Scotty paused at the green stop light and looked east and west, trying to spot the Camaro while cars behind us blew their horns for him to drive. He decided to go east and drove for a couple of blocks, looking for the car and telling me to look for it. Scotty made a U-turn and headed west for a couple of blocks, still trying to find the bright red car that had vanished. He cruised through the area's restaurants and hotel parking lot, looking for the red Camaro.

It seemed like the driver and the red car were demons sent to frighten me and harass Scotty. After exiting the freeway, the automobile vanished without any trace of the bright red vehicle. I'm sure the driver knew the area and took a side street off the main highway.

Scotty was enraged and frustrated that he couldn't find the scarlet car and said the driver had gotten over on him. My body shudders when I think of the chase and the driver hitting his brakes in the middle of the expressway, with us speeding at ninety miles per hour.

I could tell you many stories of Scotty almost getting us killed. That Monday, after returning to Madison, Scotty and I were on West Washington Avenue near the capitol. Scotty was parked illegally, as he often did. A young Madison police officer politely told Scotty he needed to move because he was in a 'no stopping, no parking' zone. The officer was not rude, disrespectful, or challenging, but Scotty perceived it that way.

"I'll move it in a minute. I'm just going inside to pick up one thing, and I'll be right out."

"Sir, you must move your vehicle now, or I will ticket you."

"Do what you need to do. I told you I would be right out."

We entered the store and came out within minutes. The officer was writing a ticket and placing it on the car as we exited the door.

Scotty shouted at the officer, limped to the car, snatched the ticket off, and handed it to the officer. "I'm not paying this. I'm leaving now. I told you I would be right out. You can tear this up."

"Sir, the ticket has been written, and I can't tear it up now. Once we've started writing a citation, we cannot rip it up." He placed the ticket back in the door.

"I'm not paying that! Call your Sergeant! I want to talk to him. I'm staying here until he comes."

We stayed in the 'no stopping, no parking' zone as the officer walked to his squad car, called his Sergeant, and waited for the Sergeant to come to the site. The Sergeant strolled to the squad car. I watched the younger officer's mouth move as he briefed his superior and pointed in our direction. The Sergeant and the policeman strolled over to our car. The older officer listened while Scotty explained why he should not have gotten a ticket.

The Sergeant nodded as Scotty talked, and after Scotty finished speaking, he said, "I understand your complaint, Mr. Brian, but my officer was correct in writing the citation. You can always fight it in court. Perhaps, get some points decreased if the commissioner doesn't dismiss the citation."

The Sergeant and the officer strolled back to the squad car, and the superior slid into his van and drove away.

Scotty remained in the 'no stopping, no parking' zone until the young policeman pulled away.

"He's a young punk! I bet he's nothing without that uniform. I want to catch him without that uniform. I would kick his butt!" Scotty started tailing the officer.

"What are you doing, Scotty? You're going to get yourself arrested."

"I'm not scared of that punk! Let him try to arrest me. It would be worth me returning to jail to kick his arrogant butt!"

The officer cruised about twenty miles per hour and knew we were following him. He turned left, and Scotty turned left. He stopped, and Scotty stopped.

Holding my breath, I prayed for God to make Scotty start the car so we could head toward home. After praying, I pleaded with Scotty to stop following a police officer. Of all the people to harass, a police officer. "This is madness, Scotty. He can arrest you for anything; it will be your word against his. And if they arrest you, they might beat you, as I hear so often happens in the jails."

"I told you I'm not scared of that punk or his buddies."

My breath and heart rate increased. "What if the officers start shooting? You might not care about being shot, but I do. I'm just an innocent bystander who happens to be in the car with a foolish man." He was so angry with the officer that he didn't hear me call him a foolish man. Otherwise, the focus would have changed from the police officer to me.

The young officer parked and sat in his squad car for ten minutes. And we sat behind him, parked in our car. Five minutes later, flashing red and blue lights and twelve to fifteen officers with weapons surrounded us. They shouted, "Step out of the car with your hands raised."

Scotty sat with his hands on the steering wheel for a few minutes and then maneuvered from the driver's side. I stood beside my door, blinking to stop sweat pellets of fear from dropping into my eyes. One of the law enforcement officers searched us for weapons and questioned our intent in following the officer. Scotty said he would only talk to the Sergeant.

A few moments later, the Sergeant returned. Scotty used his military background to create a bond with the Sergeant. His anger and aggression toward the younger officer ditched after chatting with the superior officer.

The Sergeant dismissed the other officers and chatted with Scotty for nearly an hour, reminding him that the citation was as written. He said, "I'm confident the ticket will be dismissed or reduced if you go to court."

When we left downtown and headed home, I could finally catch my breath, and my normal breathing returned.

A few blocks from home, a teen male loitered at the streetlight and started crossing when the light turned yellow.

Scotty got very irritated when pedestrians in the crosswalk slowed down after reaching the middle point, glanced at him, and then strolled at a snail's pace after making eye contact.

My pulse hammered in my neck, and my breath increased when I glanced at Scotty, sensing he was about to do something foolish.

Scotty stared at the teen as we approached the yellow light. "I don't understand why they don't cross when the light is green. I can make this light. I've got to go to the restroom." He frowned. "If he looks at me and slows down, I'm going to run him over if he doesn't move out of my way."

The young pedestrian made long strides until he got midpoint of the crosswalk. He glanced at our car, almost at the streetlight, to ensure we saw him. He slowed his pace and swaggered toward the other side. Scotty gunned the accelerator, picked up speed, and tried to hit the young man.

The teen sprinted to the curb and started shooting at our car. I screamed and ducked to the floor, praying no bullets hit the car or us. Having run the red light, Scotty sped up, and my guardian angels protected us. Not one shot hit the vehicle, and we quickly left the young man's range.

I screamed, "Your temper almost got us killed!"

Scotty said, "I was only trying to scare the punk. I knew he would hurry across the street if I sped up."

My concern was that Scotty's reflexes were not as quick and sharp as he thought, and he was not that expert of a driver. Scotty would have struck the teen if he hadn't started running. Never in a million years did I expect the kid to pull out a gun and start shooting at a moving car. I thanked God that my guardian angels were always around me. Scotty made them work extra to protect me when I was with him.

By the time we reached our neighborhood, the sun had floated behind gray clouds, twilight was approaching, and misty fog filled the atmosphere.

PSYCHOPATH OR DEMON POSSESSED?

A few weeks later, Scotty dragged into the house, wet from perspiration and talking to himself. "That DC guy is crazy! He is a downright fool. I see why they call him Death Cop."

I watched him as he lumbered into the living room, sweat rolling down his face, his top clinging to him, looking like he had just come out of a sauna. It was 40 degrees or lower outside, an unusually cold day for April, and he was sweating like it was 90-degree weather.

I hesitated in questioning him, unsure I wanted to hear what he was mumbling about, but curiosity got the best of me. "What are you talking about, and where are you coming from?" Concern wrinkled my brows as I eyed him. "I thought you were grocery shopping. How did you run into this DC man?"

Anxious and annoyed, an exasperated sigh came from his mouth as his chest heaved. "I'm telling you, I'm not afraid of too many things, and I'm not scared of any man, but that DC was creepy and had my hair standing straight up on my arms."

"What did he do that was so creepy?" I grabbed the remote from the coffee table and turned the volume down on the television, thinking I could steal a glance while I listened to Scotty.

"DC told me to meet him at some barn house, past Janesville, in the boonies. It was pitch black and dark, with no streetlights, and it started raining. He didn't give me an address to go to; he just gave me some directions and told me I'd find it. I almost turned around –"

I interrupted. "Why were you meeting DC?" I had missed the scheduling of this meeting while eavesdropping.

"That's not your business. I'm trying to tell you that the man is a maniac. Anyway, I almost turned around to come back home. Something didn't feel right. But you know me, I'm always up for a challenge, and I wasn't going to let DC outsmart me or think I was chicken." He glanced at his wristwatch. "It took me about an hour to find the darn place, but I found it. I'm glad I kept those flashlights in the car because I needed them tonight. I found the place, and it was a real barn. I was searching for a bar or someone's house, thinking they called it a barn house because it was so big."

His body shivered from the wet shirt. I grabbed a dry top and sweater and laid them on his arm.

Scotty continued talking as he changed into the dry shirt, slipped the sweater on, and plopped onto a brown liftchair facing me. "Well, after I parked on the grass and searched for the door, two young dudes came out of nowhere. They gave me the fifth degree, asked questions, and then searched and patted me down like I was one of their cronies. I told them that DC was expecting me and I wouldn't be out there in the boondocks if he hadn't invited me.

"They acted like I was lying, telling me to hop back in the car, sit tight, and not go anywhere like I would be going somewhere. There wasn't anything out there but that big barn, and those punks had my car keys."

He leaned back onto the chair. "I was beginning to become irritated by then, but I couldn't go nowhere because they had my keys." He inhaled and exhaled. "I didn't like the feel of the situation. While in the car, I slipped my 38 revolver into my secret coat pocket. They had frisked me once. I didn't think they would frisk me again once I got inside. Those thugs thought I was a stupid, scared old man. They didn't frighten me." His chest lifted several times, and he frowned. He mumbled, "This ain't my first rodeo."

Beads of sweat sparred on his forehead, and his chest still rose and fell rapidly. "The punks returned to the car about fifteen minutes later, snatched the door open, grabbed my left arm, and dragged me out. They took me into the barn. I'm talking about a real barn, stinking, with hay and farm animals. This tall, slim young man, wearing a tailormade suit in a barn, was grinning and standing before three men tied to chairs. He looked like he was in charge but didn't look like the man I met a year ago. That guy who introduced himself as DC had been shorter and stockier. This dude was a totally different man."

Scotty's breathing was back to normal now. "I started introducing myself and reminding him why I was there, and he had the gall to tell me to shut up and speak when spoken to. He didn't have the guts to look me in the face and tell me to shut up. He talked to me from the back of his head as the punks shuffled me behind him." Scotty's head shook, and he shrugged. "I wasn't sure what was going on. I didn't know if he was Death Cop or not. He wasn't the man I met last year. I should have looked at some photos when he was on the police force. Then I would have known what DC looked like. Well, I forgot to do that. I've got a lot going on."

Scotty's lips puckered as he exhaled. "Can you grab me a coke? My mouth is dry." After downing half of the soda, he crossed his right leg over his left knee and glanced at me. "This skinny guy cracked corny jokes that weren't funny and then played Russian roulette with the three men tied to the chairs. I'm telling you, that man is crazy. He made me stand for over an hour without my cane. Those thugs wouldn't let me take it in. As he played with those guys, pointing the pistol from one forehead to the other, saying, "Eeny, meeny, miny, moe, catch a traitor by the nose," his back faced me. Whenever he said moe, he pulled the trigger and then laughed diabolically, like Satan himself was in the barn, earsplitting and sending chills to my bones."

As if reliving the laugh, Scotty dropped his right leg to the floor and propped both elbows on his knees. "It was bad enough to make me stand that long with my bad knees and hip, but that idiot included me in the game." Scotty's hands went together as if praying. "The maniac turned around, pointed the gun toward my head, and pulled the trigger when he said, "Moe." It shocked and startled me, and I lost my balance and fell. DC and several other thugs in the barn cackled and gave each other high-fives like they had done something spectacular. None of them offered to help me up, not that I wanted them to."

Scotty buried his face in his hands. Instead of helping me up, DC had the nerve to ask, "'Did you doo-doo in your pants, old man?'"

"I just looked at him and didn't say a word as I struggled to my feet.

"He then started talking to me like I was someone's child. He said, "'You've been spoken to. You can talk now. What new information do you have for me about my competition?'"

"Before I could respond, he turned and started with that eeny, meeny, miny, moe, catch a traitor by the nose chant and pointed the gun at my head again. I thought about pulling my 38 out, but it was too many of them. Like a Jack Rabbit, DC U-turned and pointed the pistol toward one of the men in the chairs and pulled the trigger. He laughed that devilish crow, slapped the head of one of the men tied to the chair, and returned his attention to me. That man is a psycho! I gave him information about BM trying to take over the south territory of Madison, and he promised to visit me in the next couple of weeks. Death Cop stopped grinning and looked me over like he could tell if I was telling the truth by glaring at me. He started talking to himself while he checked the cartridges in his pistol.

"After a long pause, DC mumbled, '"So BM doesn't think Chicago is enough for him, uh?"'

"Why did you tell him that, Scotty? You don't know whether Boston wants to take over the Madison area."

"Revenge, baby. Do you want me to finish telling you or not?"

My head nodded. I was curious to hear about the man who scared Scotty Brian.

"Death Cop stared at me for a long time, but it looked like he was staring through me. I hoped that fool didn't point that pistol at me again and pull the trigger. I might not have been lucky the second time. He put that stupid grin on his face, turned his back to me again, and started his chant with the three tied-up fellows. Ten to fifteen minutes passed while I waited for him to respond, ask more questions, or tell me I could go. Fingers snapped, and two gang bangers grabbed me and dragged me to the door. "Before they opened the red barn door, DC shouted, '"Old man!"' When I turned to face him, the fool shot above my head. He slapped his thighs, thundering with laughter, turned his back toward me, and snapped his fingers again. The two punks dragged me through the door to my car and threw my car keys on the ground. Those dogs!"

Scotty growled. "They better be glad I'm older because if I were a young man, one of us would be dead."

Scotty crossed his arms in front of his chest and elevated the legs of the chair. "DC said Boston Matheson and some chick had lived together a few years ago, and BM stopped coming to Madison when the girl died." Scotty heaved and tilted his chin to his chest. "I knew that punk had been to Madison...And lived with Charlessa. Well, DC said he's had his eyes on Boston Matheson for a year."

I said, "Don't you remember Charlessa spending most of her weekends in Chicago before she died?"

Scotty frowned, and his chin tilted in my direction.

PATIENCE PAYS OFF

A few weeks later, BM called, and Scotty had the phone on speaker. "Is that home-cooked dinner offer still open, Mr. Scotty? I plan on being in your city next weekend. I'm working overtime to finish up some business this week. I will be free next weekend to spend time with you and Miss Hannah. I'll do a little business, but I want one evening with you and Miss Hannah."

I had begun to think Scotty had lost the challenge with Boston Matheson. He had been trying to manipulate BM to Madison for nearly two years. Boston didn't come at Scotty's request but was always able to smooth talk Scotty with heartfelt apologies and promises that he would make it the next time.

Scotty had the patience of Job, I must say, as it related to BM. He didn't give up trying to entice BM to Madison. And one weekend in May, it happened. The phone rang, and I answered, "Hello."

"Hello, Miss Hannah," Boston said on the other end, his smile and jovialness sounding through the phone. "I'm positive you and Mr. Scotty will not believe this, but I am actually in Madison. I didn't call ahead because I didn't want to say I was coming and have to cancel again. Is the old man home?"

"Yes, he's here. What's your favorite meal?"

"Whatever you cook, I will eat. Don't go through any trouble for me."

"It will be a good, southern meal. Tomorrow, after church, at our home. Here's Scotty." I handed the phone to Scotty. "It's Boston Matheson."

"Good evening," Scotty said, smiling. "I haven't heard from you in days. What's been going on? Business keeping you from calling, huh?"

"As a matter of fact, I have been extremely busy with my business, but I have a surprise for you."

"And what is the surprise?"

"Now, it wouldn't be a surprise if I told you, right?"

"I'm not much on surprises. I'd rather you tell me what it is than try to surprise me. I don't handle surprises very well."

"Okay, old man, I mean Mr. Scotty. I finally made it to Madison, and I am in your great city, even as I speak. I never made it for your infamous meatloaf and fried turkey, but we can meet at a restaurant tonight. If I'm still in the city, I told Miss Hannah I'd come over for Sunday dinner. Can you and Miss Hannah be ready in an hour, and I'll send Don Juan to pick you up?"

"Wait! Where are we going for dinner, and how long will you be here? We still want to cook that home-cooked meal for you. How about tomorrow evening or lunch tomorrow?"

"Let's just enjoy tonight, old man. Tomorrow isn't promised, as I've heard you say so often. We'll wait and see what tomorrow brings. Like I said, if I'm still here tomorrow, I'll have Sunday dinner with you and Miss Hannah. Don Juan will be there in an hour."

Scotty hung up the phone with a puzzled look, furrowed eyebrows, and narrowed eyes. He stopped in the hallway as he headed for the bedroom. "Get dressed, Hannah. BM is sending Don, what's his name, to pick us up for dinner in an hour."

"Where are we going so I'll know whether to dress casually or wear a dressy dress?"

"Darn if I know! You wear anything. You look like a cow in everything you wear anyway. You shouldn't even go. I'll tell BM you're on a diet and didn't want to be tempted to find the five pounds you lost."

"You are such a cruel and evil man. What you just said didn't need to be stated. I feel bad enough about all of this extra weight. I didn't want to go anyway. I was only going because I thought you wanted us to present this image to Boston Matheson. I really don't want any part of what you're trying to do. I've told you several times that I think it's wrong, and you should just forget it."

He continued with his tirade about my weight. "If you had some discipline and didn't eat everything in sight, you would lose some weight. I'm the same size I was when I first joined the military."

"Who cares?"

"What did you say?" He hobbled back into the living room, leaning on his cane, and pointed his finger in my face, touching my nose. "You'd better watch your mouth!"

Without thinking, I slapped his hand out of my face.

"Don't ever put your finger in my face again." Scotty stumbled backward, and his cane fell to the floor. He reached for the wall for support but wasn't quick enough and crashed to the floor. As I strolled to the guest bedroom, I glanced at him before stepping into the room and locking the door.

"Yeah. Take your fat butt back there and add more to that already overweight frame. I'm sure you're eating something in there. We'll deal with this issue when I get back."

While locked in the bedroom across from Scotty while he dressed, I overheard him say to someone on the phone, "The lion has arrived."

He spoke low, but I still understood him. "I will send the rendezvous point as soon as I find out where we're having dinner." He paused and continued, "I don't think the first plan will work because his goons are with him." He hesitated. "Yeah, Don Juan and most likely the other three bodyguards that stick to him like glue. The tour of the university is a no-go tonight." He hung up the phone, and I kept my ears to the door for a few more minutes before sitting back on the bed.

Scotty's first plan was for BM to have dinner at our home alone and take him on tour to show him the city.

Scotty's car gets carjacked. Scotty shoved out of the vehicle. And Boston Matheson gets kidnapped. Scotty thought he had earned BM's trust as a surrogate dad and that Boston would spend an evening with us without his bodyguards.

I planned to alert the Madison Police when I knew Scotty's detailed plan, where the meeting was, and when they hoped to carry out their scheme. I didn't want Boston killed because of a vendetta from Scotty. Without Scotty's intervention, it would be out of my hands if BM and DC quarreled. But to know that Scotty was setting up an ambush and starting a drug war was asinine. I was helpless to intervene now.

Perhaps I should have gone to dinner with them. At least I would have known where they were going and been able to alert the police. Now, I could only pray that BM was as bright and perceptive as usual and returned to Chicago without harm.

The doorbell rang, and after several rings, I surmised that Scotty was not answering it. Don Juan was at the door with a gorgeous model/actress-looking woman cuddled under his arms. I invited them into the living room, determining if his date was Black, Indian, Asian, or Spanish. She was exquisite.

After providing beverages, I entertained them while Scotty dressed. Don Juan's date was talkative, friendly, poised, and dignified. Don Juan could not keep his eyes off her and seemed more reserved and less of a jokester than when we first met him. *I think Don Juan is in love.*

After listening to Malaya chat for several minutes, I discovered she was Filipino and Black. She glanced at my outfit, "Is that what you're wearing?"

"I'm staying in and letting the men bond."

Don Juan interjected, "Boss Man is expecting both of you, Madam. He is going to be very disappointed when you don't come."

"Please give my apologies to him and tell him I'm a little under the weather and my energy level is low tonight."

Malaya chimed in. "It might boost your energy if you got out of this house. I have low energy when I stay in my house all day. And I don't feel any positive energy coming from this house. My energy level would be low, too, if I had to stay in this environment most of the time. Why don't you go and dress and...."

"Sweetheart," Don Juan interrupted, stroking Malaya's hair. "Give daddy a kiss." He glanced at me. "It's up to you, Madam. I just do what my boss tells me. I'll let the Mister explain it to him."

Scotty came out of the back. He shook hands with Don Juan and introduced himself to Malaya. She looked at Scotty, at me, at Scotty, and at me again. Her brows creased, and her nose wrinkled like she was putting lost puzzle pieces back together. She smiled. "You have a beautiful and kind wife, sir."

Scotty ignored her comment and walked toward the door. "Let's go."

I stood at the door as they walked to the BMW and watched as Don Juan opened the front door for his beautiful friend and then opened the back door for Scotty. *Um, something looks funny.* As the car pulled away, I strolled out to the porch. *It doesn't look right out here. Why is it so dark?* Thick, ghost-gray fog filled the night scene, and I could barely see the house across the street. My eyes lifted toward the streetlights. *Ah, that's the problem. All the streetlights were out, and I wondered what had happened.* I glanced up and down the cul-de-sac. *It looks eerie out here, and I'm glad I didn't go with them. I'd rather be safe in my home on a night like this.*

If this was the night Scotty hoped to ambush Boston Matheson, he couldn't have picked a better night. After re-entering the house, I phoned the energy company, and the spokesperson said streetlights were out all around the city and they were working on it. The customer service representative said service would be restored in four to five hours.

The meteorologist reported the weather had been warmer than usual for the spring season, but the temperatures dropped after dark, which caused all of the fog. They called it radiation fog and predicted it would be gone by morning once the day warmed up enough to dissipate it.

Scotty returned home around midnight and woke me up with all the noise. I pretended to be asleep because if his plans didn't go how he wanted, I would bear the brunt of his anger and frustration. He started chanting and humming phrases from his psychic book.

I whispered, "Jesus, Jesus, Jesus, Jesus, Jesus, Jesus," and Scotty abruptly stopped chanting, walked out of the bedroom, and went out to the deck. My curiosity overtook me, as usual, and I tiptoed into the living room and hid behind the curtains, peeking through the window, trying to figure out what Scotty was up to.

He mumbled, "I think I will have to kill BM myself, Charlessa. He's like a jackrabbit. He moves too fast and doesn't stay in one area long enough for me to plan anything. I called and told DC's flunky when we left the restaurant. They were supposed to corner him where they have all those one-way streets near the Capitol. The thick fog was the perfect night, and all the streetlights were out. You couldn't see anything, and the fog made visibility even worse. DC called BM on his cell while we were at the restaurant because I heard him use the name DC. I guess they met each other before tonight." He paced back and forth on the patio.

Still muttering as he paced, he stopped and stared, as if looking at someone, and said, "After leaving the eating place, we drove to Washington Avenue, and BM's three bodyguards hopped out. That big one, Don Juan, stayed in the car with us. It was funny because they took those stupid sunglasses off tonight. It was so dark and foggy that they might have been scared. We couldn't see three feet ahead of us. You couldn't distinguish anything, and I didn't know what was happening.

"BM was cool as potato salad. He chatted and laughed with me like we were still in the well-lit restaurant. I tried getting information from him, but he didn't share doo doo. A few minutes later, those three punks came back, handed something to BM, and we drove off. I don't think I can trust that Death Cop. BM probably paid him off too." Scotty's shoulders hunched, and he seemed to shrink a few inches.

I stood behind the curtain in awe, slack-jawed, and my gaze fixed on Scotty. He was talking to his dead daughter again like she was listening. I sighed as I moved away from the window. "Well, at least no one got killed tonight, and Scotty's plan backfired," I mumbled. I wondered if

BM realized what type of person Scotty was, what he was up to, and was giving him enough rope to hang himself.

I tell you the truth, Scotty would not give up. I thought after the failure in Madison, Scotty would throw his hands up in defeat. But he held on to the resentment and revenge. He kept telling me BM was a powerful drug dealer, the trucking business was a front for his drug trafficking, and he would kill Boston Matheson if that were the last thing he did before he died.

The following day, Scotty said, "BM's got the whole city of Chicago and Madison in his back pocket, that's why he seems so legit, and you never hear a tidbit about his drug business. I know because I listened to Charlessa's messages and found her journal and read it."

My eyes lifted from the book I was reading to glare at him.

He nodded. "Yeah, just like I read your diary. Charlessa wrote about some hot, rich guy pursuing her, and she was playing hard to get. Then she wrote that she liked him and might go on one date. But she didn't want to become too involved because she heard through the grapevine that his business was a front for his drug trafficking, and he was the biggest drug dealer in Chicago." His head shook. "I don't understand how she got mixed up with him when I told her to stay away from drug dealers and pimps. I warned her that it would only lead to trouble for her." A twisted smile tried to come. "She was stubborn like me and was furious that I read her journal. I bet she dated him to get back at me, or he threatened her or something."

A blank expression covered my face as I stared at him. Thoughts went through my head that she dated BM because she wanted to, but I couldn't tell Scotty that.

Scotty's patience and persistence paid off. He couldn't execute Boston Matheson through Death Cop but found another route to entangle BM. Scotty discovered that two of his young cousins in St.

Louis worked for BM's trucking company. After spending most of the summer going back and forth to St. Louis and sweet-talking his young relatives, he obtained details on how BM's operation worked and when a large shipment of narcotics was coming in from Mexico.

His cousins were Lieutenants in Boston's organization, the lowest on the totem pole, selling drugs on the streets.

Boston's structure mimicked the military, with Generals in charge in the small towns, Colonels and Majors distributing and supervising the four regions of the city, and Lieutenants selling the drugs on the streets.

BM peddled prescription drugs such as Oxycontin, Morphine, Vicodin, Demerol, Ativan, Valium, and sleeping pills. He sold uppers, downers, and all-arounders. Scotty understood the narcotics officers needed to search the truck before Boston's soldiers removed the drugs, or BM couldn't be investigated. For BM to be arrested, Boston Matheson had to be connected to the trucks. Scotty concluded that it might take him years to draw close enough to BM to kill him and was planning to pay someone in prison to shank BM.

The truck was pulled over for a moving violation in East St. Louis and searched for suspicion of carrying contraband. The first several boxes opened had only legal medical supplies in them, and the officers were about to suspend their search when one of them spotted a bulge in the lining. He hopped back onto the transporter and pulled the lining away. After grabbing a box cutter, he cut the lining from top to bottom and discovered vials and vials of narcotics taped behind the lining on both sides of the truck.

Scotty was overjoyed when the news reached him from the narcotics officers. BM was arrested without incident at his office in Chicago for suspicion of interstate drug trafficking. However, he was only held one night in jail and then released on his own recognizance. The courts delayed setting a trial date. Scotty was furious and harassed the Madison and Chicago prosecutors daily, hoping his hounding would put some fire under them to move on the case.

I prayed for Scotty to let it go and move on with his life. He had missed out on enjoying his life trying to kill and convict Boston Matheson and destroyed the little love I had left for him.

Boston Matheson's arrest was covered on the national news, highlighted as "Golden boy implicated in drug trafficking." I last heard BM fought the case as an illegal search and seizure. The narcotics officers had failed to show a search warrant before searching and tearing his truck apart.

GUILT AND SHAME

I wondered if God was trying to speak to me in my dreams because the weirdest and most frightening illusions came to me in night-mares. Like a dream I had before we married, where I felt the Holy Spirit gave me insight into the *real* Scotty. I had terrifying dreams and believed the Holy Spirit warned me about Scotty's violent nature.

Soon after Boston's arrest, I woke up screaming, swinging my arms, and gasping. My behavior was so disturbing that Scotty was concerned that something was happening to me.

Scotty shook my shoulder. "Wake up, Hannah, you were having a nightmare, and it must have been bad because you were fighting and screaming. Someone must have been attacking you." After I gained awareness and he determined I was okay and not in any physical dis-tress, he chuckled and asked, "Anybody I know?"

I stared at him for several moments, still trying to balance my bearings. *It was just a dream, and I'm awake now.* "I'm okay, Scotty. Thanks for waking me and being concerned. You can go back to sleep. I'll be fine in a minute."

After tossing from left to right and unable to fall asleep, I settled my back onto four pillows and thought about the dream. The nightmare was so frightening that my hands shook as I thought about it. It seemed more like a hallucination than a dream, as if I was outside my body watching everything happen.

In the illusion, I forgot to lock the bathroom door while showering. As I stepped out of the shower, my bath towel hanging on a hook across from me, Scotty burst into the bathroom and accused me of being a slut, sleeping around on him, and started beating me with his fists. Stunned, wet, and naked, I tried to grab my towel to protect myself from some of the blows. But Scotty had me cornered. His six-foot frame blocked the doorway, and I couldn't run past him. Even if I had been daring enough to run out of the house naked, my back was to the wall, and the windowsill too high to reach. I tried to fight back. He held my arms and kicked my shins. I screamed in pain.

When his fist started toward my face, I snatched my hands away and protected my face with my arms. His hands went for my chest. He hit my legs and thighs when I covered my chest and face with both hands. I dropped to the floor and curled into a fetal position.

When I tried kicking him, he grabbed my feet and dragged me out of the bathroom, on the cold tile, and onto the hardwood floor.

As I relived the dream, my body trembled from fear, and my hands went to my chest to calm my pounding heart while I hyperventilated. It was challenging and puzzling to ponder, but I needed to understand if God was speaking to me through my subconscious since I was hell-bent on making the marriage work.

My eyes closed, and I inhaled and exhaled several times while gazing at Scotty sleeping beside me.

In the nightmare, Scotty snatched me up from the floor by my arms and started punching me in the face, more brutal than a heavyweight boxer's punches. That's where the dream ended. One odd thing puzzled me in the nightmare: Scotty didn't use a cane and was not disabled. He was a strong, healthy, and muscular thirty-year-old.

I slipped out of bed, went to the fridge, and drank a little water before bowing down in front of my altar to pray. I asked Yahweh to give me the interpretation of that awful dream. It felt so real that my heart raced, and my body trembled as I recalled it. *Was Jehovah trying to show me something about Scotty? What did the dream mean? Scotty was not able-bodied now and couldn't beat me like that. Once I shoved him to the floor, I could run away from him.* Questions rushed through my head. *Was the dream a revelation that Scotty might try to catch me getting out of the shower and attack me? Or was it just a pizza dream and nothing to be concerned about?*

But I was concerned, and the dream perturbed me.

After the nightmare, recollections of past abuse experienced at the hand of my first husband, Beechie, resurfaced. I had forgiven Beechie and buried most of the memories, but now they returned like popping popcorn.

I couldn't go through abuse again. I wouldn't go through abuse again!

My mind started dwelling on evil imaginations. It even schemed ways to kill Scotty - drowning him in bubbling grits or steaming cooking oil, stabbing him while he slept, bludgeoning him, smothering him with a pillow as he lay in a stupor from the pain tablets and sleeping pills, and even thoughts of castrating him crept from my head.

All those thoughts were heinous fantasies. Every one of the stories reported things other women did to men that beat them—the hot grits from an article about a celebrity getting grits poured on him. The stabbing and bludgeoning from television newscasts and the castration from a worldwide story about a wife cutting her husband's male genitalia off.

But those ideas were *all* only evil imaginations. I could never have gone through with them, although Satan was slipping the thoughts into my head. Yes, I was hurt, angry, and resentful toward Scotty, but I realized all those acts were *sins* against God.

I also realized it was only a dream. But it terrified me and brought back horrible memories of past abuse and wicked ideas of getting revenge.

When I couldn't remove the upsetting dream from my head, I phoned Dr. Joyce to request her revelations.

She shared helpful knowledge, as always. "God sometimes speaks to us in dreams if we are discerning. Sometimes, it informs us we have not dealt with past issues, like abuse. Other times, He gives us opportunities to deal with hidden areas of unforgiveness, hurt, anger, and bitterness that we haven't dealt with. Our God is such a loving and caring Father that He doesn't want us carrying the heavy burdens of unforgiveness, hurt, anger, and bitterness." She paused and asked, "Does what I said make sense?"

My head nodded, and I replied, "Yes."

Dr. Joyce added, "There is also the issue of guilt and shame that you may not have dealt with."

One eyebrow lifted. *Why would I have guilt and shame? I didn't do anything wrong. I wasn't the perpetrator. I was the victim,* I thought.

I recalled the emotions after the incidences of abuse with Beechie. What emotions? I had buried those feelings so deeply that I couldn't remember how I felt.

"Hannah," Dr. Joyce called my name. "Are you okay?"

"I'm trying to remember feelings I had with my first husband. I don't recall how I felt, but I'm sure it wasn't guilt and shame." I breathed into the receiver. "I don't understand why I should feel guilt or shame."

"Take some time this week and think about your emotions when physical, verbal, or emotional abuse occurred. Stop by the office next week, and we can discuss this. Schedule an appointment so I'll have time for you."

"Okay, thanks for always being available for me, Dr. Joyce."

"I'll see you next week, then. Bye."

After disconnecting, I stared at the raindrops falling on the cars parked on the street and thought about my feelings. There was anger because I didn't deserve to be hit and abused by my spouse, who was supposed to love and protect me. I sighed and rested my chin on my hands. I didn't think I had guilt and shame. Why would I?

A slight stirring started in my stomach, traveling down my legs and running back to my heart. I leaned back and looked up toward heaven. Perhaps I did feel a little bit ashamed. My friends' spouses treated them like queens, and my man treated me like a punching bag.

My head nodded. Yes, I guess I was ashamed. I never told anyone because of the embarrassment of admitting that my husband beat and abused me, and I continued to live with him. Guilt? Guilt? I nibbled my bottom lip while rubbing both eyebrows. Beechie always said that I provoked him to hit me because of something I did or didn't do. Maybe I did sense guilt thinking I was not a good wife.

Perhaps I accepted blame, believing I provoked him and caused him to hit me - saddled with Stockholm syndrome while with Beechie. Possibly, I felt guilt and shame believing I was not a good mother or committed wife. I had never thought of myself as having hidden feelings of shame or guilt, but perhaps I did.

My jaw rested on one hand as I dug into the past about my relationship with Scotty. I had lost my personhood being with Scotty.

My spirit and confidence had shrunk to the size of a mouse. There was indeed guilt and shame because I didn't stand up to him and continued to accept the verbal insults.

ENCOUNTER WITH THE DEMONIC SPIRIT

As I shoveled back to earlier times, I buried my face in my hands, and my shoulders slumped from shame. I was in such denial with Scotty that my eyes, mind, and spirit were closed to his hateful and unloving behaviors. My head said I didn't have to deal with them if I didn't acknowledge them. Unfortunately, my body suffered the consequences when I ignored the spiritual and emotional breaking.

The stress created terrible repercussions for my physical body. After we separated, my health slowly recovered, but the pressure nearly destroyed me.

I endured his abuse until I finally got the courage and confidence to leave and divorce Scotty.

Before I married Scotty, I was mindful of the signs of mistreatment. But after marriage, I ignored them, *blinded* by Satan's aberrations.

The scales had fallen from my eyes, and my spiritual sight was now lucid—no more clouded vision like cataracts on my eyes. I was no longer blind. For two torturous years, I stayed in the *Wormwood Marriage*, and it almost killed my spirit and my flesh.

Too many times, I was put down and embarrassed in front of my family. Scotty was such an enigma. The few times we spent with his family; he treated me better in their presence than in the company of my family. I thought he'd want to deceive my family into thinking he was treating me well. But Scotty talked harsher, shouted, and spoke demandingly when with my relatives.

Scotty was so peculiar. The things he should have been doing, he didn't do, and the things he should not have been doing, he did.

For instance, he attacked me in front of my sisters while at a graduation party for my great-nephew. Coincidently, one of my cousins is married to a man with the same last name as my ex-husband. When Scotty noticed the name Solomon Cotton on the program, his countenance changed from chatty to cranky. He had dominated the discussion until the hostess dropped the programs in the middle of our table. After reading the program, he glanced around the room as if searching for someone.

My spirit felt the malevolent spirits emanating from him.

He grumbled, low enough for me to hear but not the others. "Your ex-husband is at this affair?"

My eyes widened, and I leaned away from him. "Of course not. Beechie doesn't even live in the city."

"That don't mean nothing. He could have taken planes, trains, buses, and cars." He looked around the dining hall again.

The demonic spirit grew stronger and stronger as the celebration progressed. Scotty's jaws clenched, and his frame seemed to expand, a musty odor suddenly coming from him in my direction. He fidgeted throughout the program, not talking to me or anyone else at our table.

After the benediction, Scotty leaned on the table to get up, snatched his cane, and headed toward valet parking. My five sisters followed us, and we stood outside talking while waiting for the attendant to bring our cars.

A few minutes later, my cousin and her husband, Solomon Cotton, came out, handed their ticket to an attendant, and waited for their car. When Scotty heard the last name, he assumed it was my ex-husband and didn't wait for introductions. In my mind, I swear Scotty turned green, and horns protruded from his forehead when I glanced at him.

He growled at me, nodding his head toward the other waiting area. "Let's go stand over there. It's too crowded here."

As he made the statement, I was greeting my cousins and didn't respond fast enough for him. He grabbed my jacket in the front and snarled. "I said, let's stand over there!"

When I snatched away, my sisters reacted instantly, lining up like toy soldiers between Scotty and me. As he stared into ten pairs of eyes, Scotty realized what he had done.

Ashley ordered, "Go inside, Hannah."

My cousins glanced at us, and Elana waved them off, indicating she had it under control.

I stood motionless behind my sisters, looking at Scotty, trying to read him. Elana opened her mouth to speak but instead spread her left and right arms in front of the other four as if to protect them. Scotty growled like a giant bear as a black mist drifted from his body, and a distinct musty and musky odor flowed into our nostrils. It was the same smell at home when his hands bawled into fists, and I thought he would strike me.

Scotty said in a strident, dead voice, "THE HUSBAND RULES OVER HIS WIFE, AND SHE IS TO SUBMIT TO HIM."

Still frozen in my spot, I glanced at Scotty as his frame enlarged and curved.

Elana lifted her head, glared at Scotty, and said, "I bind you in the name of Jesus." She spoke with authority. "I plead the Blood of Jesus over us.

> *"For our struggle is not against human foes, but against cosmic powers, against the authorities and potentates of this dark age, against the superhuman forces of evil in the heavenly realms"* Ephesians 6: 12 (REV).

Scotty's eyes focused on Elana, and he howled like an animal. He mumbled some unintelligible words and stood staring at Elana. The valet approached and told Scotty his car was ready. He stared at me without saying a word, jutted his jaw forward, twisted his neck from left to right, and stood straighter. He frowned, looked at Elana over his eyeglasses, and walked to the car. I waited for Scotty to demand that I come. He stumbled behind the steering wheel and drove off.

Elana turned, pulled me into her chest, and held me tight. "You are spending the night with me, Hannah. You will not be safe if you go home tonight. We'll deal with Scotty Brian tomorrow. I'm sure he'll be apologetic and different tomorrow."

"Why was he howling like that?" Kameron asked.

"And what was that stinking smell?" asked Tarrin.

Ashley's eyes narrowed, and her brows furrowed. "What happened, Elana? Did we miss something?"

Elana pushed us to a corner and whispered. "Scotty is full of demons, and I saw one of the big ones tonight. It stood behind him, about 8 feet tall, dark and hairy, like a grizzly bear. It looked ferocious and angry. That's why he was growling like an animal." Her head shook. "It was a dreadful, frightening-looking creature with a head the size of three men, large, bulging, red eyes, and huge flaring ears. The creature was tall and big, like a giant bear, but more vicious and monstrous than a bear. The demon was growling and reaching for Hannah with paws like a cat and long, curved nails."

"Wow!" Kameron exclaimed. "Have you ever seen it before, Hannah?"

My legs trembled like flowing water, and I shook like I was having a seizure. I tried to be brave and hold back the tears, but they began streaming down my cheeks like Niagara Falls.

My sisters hugged me, all talking simultaneously, telling me everything would be all right.

Elana said, "You belong to Christ Jesus." She held my hand. "You're going home with me, and we can develop a plan tomorrow."

HOLY SPIRIT POWER

At 6 a.m. the following morning, Scotty called Ashley, Kameron, Tarrin, Christy, and Elana.

When her landline rang, Elana put the phone on speaker so that I could hear.

Scotty said in a low voice, "Hannah didn't come home last night. Is she with you? I'm worried because that's not like her not to come home."

His voice was nothing like the previous night.

Elana was polite but firm. "She spent the night with me last night. We would not let her go home with you the way you were acting."

His voice elevated, and his tone hardened. "What do you mean, the way I was acting? I wasn't acting any differently than the rest of you fools."

"That's exactly why Hannah is here with me. You tried to attack her last night."

"You're a big liar, Elana! Let me speak to Hannah!" Elana pretended to hand me the phone. "It's Scotty."

"Hello...." I said.

He shot into me before the hello was out of my mouth good. "Why did you spend the night at Elana's? Why didn't you come home last night? I wouldn't put it past Elana to have a man over there for you. You're a big hypocrite, Hannah. What type of wife spends the night away from home and doesn't let her husband know."

"You were a big jerk, Scotty, worse than usual last night. You grabbed me in the front of my jacket and tried to drag me before they stepped in."

"You and Elana have gotten together with this lie. It won't work with me because I know you're lying. I've got more sense than to attack you in front of your family. If you don't want to be married to me anymore, just say so. Don't play games and lie about it!"

He didn't remember the incident from last night. The demonic spirits had obsessed and controlled him, and he was unaware of what had happened. "It happened, Scotty, whether you believe us or not. I *don't* want to be married to a man that I'm afraid to live in the same house with."

His voice softened and lowered. "We need to talk, Hannah. Don't make any rash decisions because of one incident. Come home, and we can talk about it like two mature individuals."

"It is not a rash decision Scotty, and it isn't based on one incident. Our marriage has been like hell on earth since it started. We're two strangers living in the same house and sharing the same bed. You know that we don't communicate, we don't have sex, and we rarely do anything together. I was surprised that you went to the celebration last night. You've been taking vacations with your female friends and spend most of your time with them." I exhaled into the receiver. "I'm tired, Scotty. Drained."

"Let's talk about this when you get home. I'll come to pick you up."

"No. I'll get Elana to bring me home."

After I hung up the phone, Elana sat beside me on the sofa. "Hannah, I'm not trying to run your life, and you have to make up your own mind, but I don't think you'll be using godly wisdom if you return to that house. I don't understand how you can sleep peacefully next to him after last night." Her mouth twisted. "I wish you could have seen the demon behind him last night, and I'm sure he has more than one of them living in him."

She looked down and away from my curious eyes. "I should have followed the Holy Spirit and told you how I felt before you married him, but I didn't want to butt in. You seemed so happy to marry him, so I figured, who am I to judge? He was too old for you. You were unequally yoked spiritually, physically, and educationally. Hannah, you were out of his league but couldn't see it." She touched my hand and gazed up at me.

My head tilted as I tried to blink back the approaching tears.

"Why don't I call the other sisters, and we'll all fast for the rest of the day and ask God to speak clearly to you."

"That sounds fine," I said, my shoulders slumped and chin to my chest. "I know what I should do and what I want to do, but I'm scared Scotty may do something crazy."

Elana placed one hand on my forehead and the other on my belly. "We bind that spirit of fear, in the name of Jesus! And we'll add casting out fear to our fast too. Remember II Timothy, seventh verse (KJV):

> *"For God has not given us the spirit of fear; but of power,*
> *and of love, and of a sound mind."*

My sisters and I only drank water and prayed for the whole day. Scotty called every fifteen minutes, asking when I would be home.

Frustrated with answering the phone, Elana let the calls go to voice mail, which made Scotty more agitated.

"I know you're there! Elana, you're a dog! Hannah, why are you letting her do this to us? She's just jealous because she doesn't have a man and trying to keep you from having one. She will win, too, if you don't get home soon."

He called right back. "Hurry home, Hannah. I'm not going anywhere until I look at your beautiful face. I didn't realize how much I missed you until now. It's so quiet in this house without you."

While I listened to his sweet but non-apologetic messages, I reflected on my desire to peep into the spiritual dimension. I thought about Elana's description of the demon in Scotty. I had been praying to be filled with the power to fight demons and command them to come out in Jesus' name, but hearing Elana describe what she visualized in the spiritual realm standing behind Scotty made me have second thoughts. I didn't think I was as ready to do spiritual warfare as I had imagined.

After ending our water fast, Kameron, Tarrin, Christy, Ashley, and Elana escorted me to my home to support me while I told Scotty I was ending our marriage. I'd accepted that it was not a God-ordained marriage anyway.

When we entered the house, Scotty was sweet as apple pie, holding the door open and smiling. "What happened last night that you are so upset?" He reached for my hand, and I backed away.

I described his behavior after the graduation celebration with my sisters' corroboration: "It's not just what happened last night, Scotty. It's the whole marriage. I think...I think it would be best for you and me if we go our separate ways. You can stay here until you find another place, and I'll move in with one of my sisters until you're gone."

He tried convincing me that I was making an ungodly decision, that God didn't like divorce, and I would be living as an adulteress if I divorced him because he was not remarrying again. "You'll still be my wife." After seeing that his deceptions and manipulations were ineffective, he threatened me.

My sisters were already interceding for me while I talked with Scotty. I heard Elana say, "Pray more fervently. The demon is beginning to raise his ugly head."

Scotty's appearance changed. His face contorted, his voice deepened, his eyes bucked, and he snarled and growled like the animal the night before. Me and my sisters headed for the front door.

Scotty stood in front of it; his eyes focused on me.

"YOU'RE NOT GOING ANYWHERE!" He howled like a wolf. "I TOLD YOU IT'S NOT OVER UNTIL I SAY IT'S OVER." He grew taller and more prominent as we stared. The same musty and musky odor from the night before drifted into our noses.

Elana shouted, "Pray in the Spirit!"

Six voices prayed in the spirit, calling out to God, pleading the Blood of Jesus, and calling the name of Jesus. Scotty started speaking louder in unintelligible languages, masking our prayers. He stepped toward us, his focus off of me and now on Elana.

Elana stayed positioned with her back straight and head high, not demonstrating fear. She continued praying, staring into Scotty's eyes. The demonic spirit tried to eliminate the most vital link and then overpower the rest of us. We prayed louder than Scotty and called the name of Jesus louder! We pled the Blood of Jesus louder!

As Scotty moved toward us, he walked tall and straight without his cane. His gaze switched from Elana toward me.

While I prayed, the Holy Spirit took control, and all fear left. I shouted, "I command you, in the name of Jesus Christ of Nazareth, to leave this house now!" I spoke firmly and confidently without taking my eyes off Scotty.

We continued praying with power and authority, watching Scotty's frame grow more prominent, taller, and grotesque. The dreadful, frightening creature with a head the size of three men, large, bulging, red eyes, and substantial flaring ears growled at me. His cat paws with long, curved nails stretched toward me. The darkness overshadowed him, and his frame increased even more, growing larger and larger and taller and taller.

The previous night, the demon discovered Elana could see him but was startled when I also saw the monstrous, serpentine creature for what it was. We understood it wasn't Scotty standing before us but the evil spirits he allowed to enter and live in him.

Like commandos on the front lines, we stood and prayed collectively with boldness and courage. We believed the God we served powers was much more significant than any potential that Scotty's little god and satanic entourage could muster.

I spoke with boldness and authority, never taking my eyes off Scotty, "I command you, in the name of Jesus Christ of Nazareth, to leave this house now!" I sounded like a scratched disk playing the same verse over and over and over again.

The giant, dark, hideous image no longer resembled Scotty or any human. He moved faster towards us, howling and growling like a wounded animal, still looking at me. When the creature was about two feet away, and his shadow covered us like an umbrella, he wrenched and stopped as if jolted with an electrical current.

The creature pushed forward with his body, acting like he had bumped into an impenetrable wall. He snarled and howled and glanced from left to right several times. The demon glared at Elana, then me, and suddenly started whimpering like a puppy.

Jehovah had demonstrated His magnificent power, as we *knew* He would. Yahweh surrounded us with His hedge of protection and showed Satan that he had no power against those who belonged to God.

While the beast struggled to escape the invisible barrier, his vast, horrendous image disappeared. Scotty stood before us looking like he had been through a wringer washer, beaten and battered, clothes ripped, and sweat dripping.

Scotty's head bowed, shoulders slumped, and he stepped to the side. "This is your house. You don't have to leave. I'll leave. I'll have Moses come get my stuff if you pack it up for him." He grabbed his cane, leaning on it with his right hand, picked his jacket off the chaise, and put it on. Before walking out the door, he took the house, garage, and keys to my car off his key ring and sat them on the kitchen table.

TRUTH REVEALED

G od has His way of revealing the truth to us if we are open to receiving it. After Scotty and I had separated, I was leaving the local library and bumped into a board member of the organization of which he was chairman. We chatted briefly, and as I walked away, Mrs. Hayes asked how Scotty was doing.

My lips pressed together while an unwanted frown wrinkled my brows. I wasn't sure if this lady was sincere or just nosey. *His board members will eventually find out,* I thought. "I'm not sure. We're separated and in the process of getting a divorce," I said in a dead, unemotional tone.

"It's about time! I was amazed when you married him and more amazed that you stayed with him so long."

My eyes widened, and I stepped closer to her. I was astonished to hear her say that because we only knew each other through Scotty, and she was not a friend of mine.

She continued having her say, ignoring the astonished look on my face. "Mr. Brian has been paying the mortgage for a young lady who lives in the same condominium as my sister."

My head tilted. "How do you know all of this? We're getting a divorce, but I'd still like to know that I didn't imagine some of the things that happened in our marriage. If that's true, it would explain many things for me."

"I first saw her when she came to a board meeting with Mr. Brian as his guest. He said he was recruiting her to the board and wanted her to sit in on a meeting and meet some board members. She sat in on one meeting but came to several and hung outside. I'm sure you've seen her. The gal never joined our board but was at most fundraising events. She is tall, has a nice figure, and is beautiful. She has black hair and wears it in a short bob." Mrs. Hayes paused and studied my face. "She was about your complexion but younger, in her thirties, I'd say."

The description sounds like the lady stalking us at Whole Foods. Tall, shapely, and attractive with a short black bob.

"Anyway, my sister, the condo association's treasurer, asked me to help her recount the money several times. Mr. Brian wrote multiple checks for her mortgage with his name and address on the bill. When I asked my sister if you all lived in the condo, she said he might as well because he's there every day. The unit was listed in that home wrecker's name."

Speechless and catatonic, I stood frozen and transfixed, wanting to move away, but my legs would not obey.

The chatterbox continued. "I visit my sister daily and would watch Mr. Brian there with that Delilah." One hand went to her hip. "Plenty of single men are out there, so there's no justification for her messing with a married man. I ran into him several times, and he acted like nothing was happening. He reminded me he was trying to recruit her for our board and talked like she was just a friend. Maybe she was." Her mouth twisted. "But I don't know what type of friendship where a married man pays the mortgage for a single woman and spends every day with her."

The silence between us seemed like forever. Still immobile, emotions of hurt, shame, and guilt pummeled me. Miss Blabbermouth was so busy venting her anger and frustration she overlooked the discomfort and pain drowning me. Tears pooled in the corner of my eyes until a tear dropped to my cheek.

"Oh, baby, I'm so sorry," Mrs. Hayes said, stepping to console me. "I thought you knew and just put up with it. I am so very sorry for opening my big mouth."

I swiped the tears with the knuckles of my index fingers, held my chin up, and said, "No. That's okay. I appreciate you telling me. I did ask how you knew all of this, and now I know. It hurts, but at least it's given me a clearer understanding of some issues, and I can put some closure to many things. I'll be okay. Thank you."

FREE AT LAST

L ike it happened yesterday, I remember a warning from the Holy Spirit from the speaker at a women's conference several days before Scotty spotted me.

After leaving the spiritual retreat, joy, optimism, boldness, and pride filled my chest.

While we gathered our wraps, purses, and belongings, the keynote speaker spoke into the microphone, "You ladies are feeling good now, with the presence of the Holy Spirit filling this room and all of us in agreement and on one accord. You will be alone when you leave here, and Satan will come at you like a roaring, hungry lion with temptations. Keep your prayer life strong, stay in God's Word, and stay in fellowship with other believers."

Shirley and I paused and waited for the speaker to finish her departing remarks.

"Our enemy and deceiver, Satan, will be waiting to trap you because of the information you've gained by attending this conference. As I said in my opening remarks, he didn't want you to be here, which is why many of you had problems with vehicles, babysitting, jobs, and spouses." She smiled. "It has been a pleasure celebrating the Lord with you, and I pray for peace over you." She waved her hands back and forth in the air as we left the auditorium.

Back then, I thought, *Satan can't tempt me. I'm hip to his games. I'm sold out to Jesus, and I'm not interested in a man at this time in my life. I just want to get to know Christ better and get closer to Him.* I felt invincible and like I had a wall of protection around me that would keep me from yielding to temptation.

To summarize, Scotty noticed me a week later at the theater outing with my friends and initiated his plan to get me as his wife. He caught me when I felt good about being a Christian but naïve because I believed God would handle everything. I thought if I handed my problems over to Jehovah, I didn't need to do anything but pray. My ignorance gave the devil a foothold, and he set up a stronghold in my life with Scotty Brian.

I made the mistake of giving Satan an inch, and he stole a mile. While experiencing the optimism of Christianhood, the devil sneaked in and convinced me that Scotty would be my mate; he just needed a supportive and compassionate wife. I believed everyone had good characteristics, and Christians needed to search for them. So, I dug for the good in Scotty and found favorable qualities. But his negatives far outweighed his positives.

The truth is, I was Bedeviled and bedazzled by Scotty's bluster and charm and went into the relationship with my spiritual eyes wide shut, throwing all common sense out the window.

After blaming Scotty for all of my problems and everything that went wrong in our marriage, with Dr. Joyce's assistance and Aunt Lucy's wisdom, I forced the courage to *look* inside myself. Deceiving myself into believing I was a faithful, submissive, Christian woman, I played the excellent *martyr* role. Again, deluding myself, I portrayed

Hannah as the perfect Christian, not complaining and taking the abuse because Jesus said, *"We must bear our own cross."* So I told myself, "Scotty was my cross to bear."

Once the cat was out of the bag, having kept most of my marital abuse problems secret, my Aunt Lucy visited from Lakeview, Arkansas, to support me. When I picked her up at the train station, I was surprised but delighted that my bashful niece, Bernadette, accompanied her. Dette, as we called her, one of my oldest brother's children, moved to Tennessee from Arkansas after some traumatic incidences in her life. For several years she stopped hanging around the family and worked from home.

On the drive home from the train station, a scolding came. "Baby, you should have told me about Scotty's abuse earlier, so I could have prayed him out of your house sooner." Aunt Lucy smiled, and her eyes twinkled. "But God is good! And everything works out right in His timing."

I nodded and changed the subject, knowing I'd get more advice for the next two weeks, and glanced at my niece in the rearview mirror. "Dette, I'm so happy you got out of the house."

Bernadette sat in the back, reading a book. She glanced up, offered a close-lipped smile, and returned to her reading.

I mouthed to Lucy, "She hasn't come out of the shell yet?"

Lucy's head shook. "I'm glad you woke up and listened to God, Hannah. God don't remove people from our lives that He didn't bring into our lives. When you married that man, you invited the demonic spirits into your home."

She stared at me to ensure I was listening. "And you was responsible for evicting them demons. Apparently, you was slack in protecting your spiritual self and gave the devil an opportunity to stick his foot in your life."

My head bobbed. "I let my guard down for an instant. Satan slipped over-confidence into my spirit when I left a women's conference a week before I met Scotty."

Lucy twisted her head to look at Bernadette. "You okay back there, Dette?"

I gazed into my rearview mirror.

Bernadette's head nodded. "Yes, ma'am. I'm good."

"Okay, I wanna make sure you're glad you came to help me."

Lucy's gaze turned toward me. "I know divorce is hard, especially the second one. That's why I'm here. You understand it wasn't all your husband's fault, right?"

My lips pressed together, and my eyebrows wrinkled, although I tried to hide my reaction.

"It takes two to make or break a marriage. You told me on the phone that you weren't honest with your husband about your feelings."

My head nodded again, and I glanced at Aunt Lucy and back to the road. "I feared his reprisal, revenge, and rejection. I was terrified to tell him my truth and scared of his verbal and emotional threats."

I looked at Dette in the rearview mirror. "I have fear issues, like you, Dette. But mine was mostly insecurity in my relationship with men."

Bernadette shrugged, returned her eyes to her book, changed her mind, and glanced at me. "But I'm afraid of everything, Aunt Hannah."

A prophetic word popped into my mouth. "Dette, I see you as a great woman of faith. And defeating satanic forces in the devil's realm."

A smile crossed Bernadette's face. "Granddad said the same thing when I was eight."

Lucy looked at me. "I've got two weeks to chat about your marriage. Tell me what we're looking at as we pass these buildings."

Aunt Lucy was a mighty woman of God. During her two-week visit, she prayed and counseled me daily.

During the following days, Auntie encouraged, but she also listened. While internalizing one of Lucy's statements, I said, "You know, Auntie, looking back, perhaps, even a little jealousy of my girlfriends and their husbands' relationships prompted me to go through with the wedding."

My lips twisted to one side. "Once yoked with Scotty, panic made me stay with him, fearing he would kill me before he let me leave him."

Aunt Lucy nodded in understanding.

Ten days later, while enjoying breakfast with Auntie and Dette before taking them to the train station, a revelation came, and I shared it with my guests. "I didn't realize it, but I had some insecurity and abandonment issues, which may have contributed to my staying in the insane relationship with Scotty for so long. As a professional nurse, I displayed self-assuredness. But confidence flew out the window in personal relationships with the opposite sex. For fear they wouldn't love or want me, I tried to please men by metamorphosing into what they wanted me to be."

Aunt Lucy said, "Baby, I'm glad you realize you're God's creation, fearfully and wonderfully made, and you have much to contribute to a relationship being yourself."

On the solo drive from the train terminal, after much deep soul-searching, I acknowledged, admitted, and took responsibility for my part in the dysfunctional relationship. I repented of my misgivings—pride, selfishness, fear, doubt, and lack of faith.

Back home, as I settled on my knees before my altar, I remembered that Satan had not changed his methods for thousands of years. He still used three powerful tactics to entice Christians away from God to create an opening for him and his imps to sneak in - Lust of the flesh, the lust of the eyes, and the pride of life:

> *"For all that is in the world, the lust of the flesh, and the lust of the eyes, and the pride of life, is not of the Father, but is of the world"* I John 2:16 (KJV).

When I took my eyes off Jesus for a second, focused on the world's enticements a little too long, Satan sneaked in like a thief. He is the little god of this *world* and controls everything.

With the emotional and verbal mistreatment before we married, my family and friends questioned why I married Scotty.

Most were even more bewildered that I had stayed with him so long. Besides being bedeviled and bamboozled by him, he could also be charming when he knew I was hurt or angered by something he said.

He never apologized but became agreeable to my suggestions, did extra things around the house, brought my favorite dishes home, or bought a surprise gift. I felt this was his way of apologizing and never viewed it as manipulation until my spiritual eyes opened.

When he was pleasant and agreeable for a season, I thanked God for answering my prayers since I was praying for Jehovah to change Scotty and save our marriage.

After our separation and while reviewing my journal, my head nodded, and a few tears dripped as I agreed with family and friends that I must have been *crazy* to go through what I did with Scotty during the courtship and still marry him.

The Holy Spirit responded expeditiously when the devil planted the idea that I was *crazy*.

"Satan planned to make you think you were crazy by causing fear, confusion, frustration, and doubt when you couldn't hear God's voice. Satan's tactics have not changed since the beginning of time. Since Adam and Eve, Lucifer's temptations have been the lust of the eyes, the flesh, and the pride of life. He gets us in bondage with soul ties and strongholds. Husbands and wives have soul ties, as they should. But somewhere along the way, your soul tie took root and became a stronghold in your life.

"You opened the door for Satan to enter through the lust of the flesh when you were intimate with Scotty before marriage. Even though you still belonged to Jesus Christ, when you returned to the sin of fornication, if only for that one time, you opened the door for your old behaviors, attitudes, and desires to enter, and along came other demonic spirits."

After asking God for specific qualities in my mate, I settled for less instead of waiting on God. Warned several times by the Holy Spirit that Scotty was not the mate I had prayed for, I chose to obey my feelings and follow my thoughts, making myself suitable in my own eyes.

I closed my eyes and waited for the Holy Spirit to speak more to my spirit. *"You allowed the devil to enter your spirit. He does not play fair and is a liar and a deceiver. After his little imps entered, he put his foot in the opening and set up a foothold, so they could come and go as they pleased and bring other demonic spirits to fill up your spiritual house. The little imps, being evil spirits, settled in and became comfortable. They brainwashed you with negative thoughts, emotions, and attitudes and established a fortress in your spiritual house.*

"The imps began torturing you with fear, confusion, frustration, and doubt making you unable to hear the voice of God. The longer you stayed in the relationship, the stronger the imps became, and the citadel developed foundations that burrowed deeply into your soul and spirit. When you repented, showed genuine remorse for your disobedience, and renounced everything associated with Satan and his imps, the fortress fell, the devils evicted, and the door slammed on Satan's foot."

I dabbed the dribbling tears wetting my cheeks. My faith wasn't powerful enough to wait on God to send my life partner. I decided I could manipulate Jehovah into healing Scotty, removing the mistrust and wickedness, and changing him into my perfect mate. I believed love could conquer everything, and if I loved Scotty with the love of Christ and prayed for him and our marriage, things would change.

I focused on what Scotty could become in the Lord – a godly, faithful, loving, devoted man of God who treated his spouse as the Bible states he should instead of what he revealed.

I repented being a confessing Christian and not a *believing* Christian. Christianity is a *faith* religion, meaning we practice our spirituality based on what we believe, not what we visualize or experience.

I demonstrated little faith and obedience regarding Scotty. Unconsciously, I decided I had been single long enough, and if God didn't send me the man I prayed for by a specific date, I would choose my own, which is what I did. As it was happening, I didn't comprehend this decision.

Still, after repenting and acknowledging my self-centeredness and disobedience, the Holy Spirit opened my spiritual eyes and mind so I could understand how I had been rebellious and disobedient. Bedeviled by Scotty and focused on him, I completely missed my participation in the scenario. I blundered on how my doubt, selfishness, and disobedience to the Holy Spirit played an important part.

It was much easier to point the finger at someone else than to look within at my imperfections. Talking about Scotty's bizarre behavior was less threatening, frightening, and challenging than dealing with my own issues. Sure, Scotty was demon-possessed, but a spirit-filled, Christ-led child of God should never have become yoked with a child of darkness.

Christians should always be on guard because our enemy, the devil, seeks someone to devour. That's why we need to put on the whole armor of God – morning, noon, and night. Then we will be prepared to fight the devil with the power of God's might.

Ephesians 6: 10-17 (KJV) states,

"Finally my brethren, be strong in the Lord, and in the power of His might. Put on the whole armor of God that ye may be able to stand against the wiles of the devil. For we wrestle not against flesh and blood, but against principalities, against powers, against the rulers of the darkness of this world, against spiritual wickedness in high places. Wherefore take unto you the whole armor of God, that ye may be able to withstand in the evil day, and having done all, to stand. Stand therefore, having your loins girt about with truth, and having on the breastplate of righteousness; and your feet shod with the preparation of the gospel of peace; above all, taking the shield of faith, wherewith ye shall be able to quench all the fiery darts of the wicked. And take the helmet of salvation, and the sword of the Spirit, which is the word of God; praying always with all prayer and supplication in the Spirit, and watching thereunto with all perseverance and supplication for all saints."

Before Scotty, I didn't consistently pray to put on the whole armor of God. I now pray Ephesians 6:10-17 the first thing in the morning, mid-day, and before bedtime. It is amazing how the scriptures become much more meaningful and have a deeper meaning after you've been through a storm.

While doing spring cleaning, I found the oddest contraptions hanging around the house that I didn't remember seeing before—plastic water-filled bags taped to each outside window. Upside-down horseshoes shouted at me from high above the arch of the front and back doors. Huge, clear bags of dirt were in the back of each closet and the basement. My spiritual eyes were lucid, and I could now eye the gadgets. Before we married, I threw his book of curses in the trash, but after moving into my house, I had not spotted the bags of hanging water, horseshoes, or bags of dirt I believe had something to do with the occult.

When I married Scotty, I anointed my home with blessed oil weekly. Looking back, I only anointed the inside of the house, not the outside, and didn't anoint the closets or basement. While I prayed to cast the demonic and evil spirits out of my home, Scotty had voodoo and idol worship objects hanging to keep the evil spirits and sickness inside the house. I burned everything that belonged to Scotty and now anoint the outside door posts, top posts, inside posts, and every window with the protection of the Holy Spirit.

While we were married, I discovered Scotty resumed his daily visits to his psychic but thought it only affected his spirituality. I didn't recall him dabbling in voodoo and satanic worship. I should have suspected something when he kept trying to bring Charlessa back from the dead. The stronger one lived in me, and I didn't believe Scotty could curse me with the Blood of Jesus covering me.

Truthfully, I suspected Scotty failed to deal with some mental health issues. I never imagined he was dealing with the occult at such a deep level. He still went to church every Sunday, every Tuesday, and every Friday, so I couldn't understand how he could be in the presence of a Holy God so often, and demonic spirits still possess him.

I'm not sure if he ever brought Charlessa back. As I said earlier, I often came home and heard him talking to her. I didn't go in the room, so I don't know if she was there as a demonic spirit or in his mind and spirit. I'll never know, and I don't care to know. It may be possible. Those evil spirits are powerful and can create demons just as Godly spirits manifest angels.

The story in the Bible about the seven sons of Sceva came to mind. One *evil* spirit in *one* man whipped the clothes off of seven men. One evil spirit! That shows us that those evil spirits are powerful.

> *"There were seven sons of Sceva, a Jewish chief priest, who were doing this, when the evil spirit responded, 'Jesus I recognize, Paul I know, but who are you?' The man with the evil spirit flew at them, overpowered them all, and handled them with such violence that they ran out of the house battered and naked"* Acts 19: 15-16 (REV).

I also don't know if Scotty ever met that Death Cop character again. That DC guy was someone Scotty was deathly afraid of. When he came home that night after meeting Death Cop, he looked terrified. After we separated, someone beat Scotty like a savage near his mistress's condominium. Circulating rumors said DC discovered Scotty was trying to use him to kill BM, and Death Cop sent his posse to kill Scotty.

While at the library, I bumped into Mrs. Hayes again, who said four cars blocked Scotty as he turned into the condo complex where he lived with his mistress. Sixteen young men jumped out of the four vehicles, wearing army gear and boots, smashed in his car windows, and snatched Scotty out of his automobile. Several men held Scotty up while the rest clobbered him, kicked him, used judo techniques, and beat him with clubs.

As she phoned the police, they dropped him to the ground and pounded him more. She said the men were precise, systematic, and swift, accomplishing their job within minutes and vanishing before the police arrived. A condo owner driving into the complex also spotted the attack and called 911 from her cell phone.

Miss Chatterbox said blood was everywhere, and she thought Scotty was dead.

Astonishingly, Scotty survived the attack. The paramedics arrived within six minutes, resuscitated him, and rushed him to the closest hospital, where they took him to intensive care. He had several surgeries due to damaged internal organs. Scotty needed a ventilator and kidney dialysis three times a week and stayed in intensive care for months. The last time I heard, he was in a specialty hospital for patients needing ventilator care and receiving dialysis treatments.

REPENTANCE WAS MY SALVATION

Repentance was the key for me. I had to repent of my sins against God and Scotty. It took some praying and soul-searching to admit I had played a role in the ungodly relationship.

Just as Job in the Bible had to pray for his friends before the Lord restored everything twofold, I prayed for Scotty. I could not be restored unless I forgave Scotty and prayed for him.

> *"And the Lord turned the captivity of Job when he prayed for his friends; also the Lord gave Job twice as much as he had before"* Job 42:10 (KJV).

I also needed to forgive myself.

> *"Repentance and rest is your salvation, in quietness and trust is your strength, but you would have none of it"* Isaiah 30:15 (NIV).

For weeks, repentance, repentance, repentance twirled around in my head until I fell to my knees and apologized to Yahweh.

After a while, everything I went through seemed like a dream, an awful nightmare that I couldn't awaken from. Those dreams where you cry out for help, but nothing comes out of your mouth, those horrors where you move your body to turn over but feel paralyzed from the neck down, unable to breathe.

For two years, I experienced a living nightmare. After repentance, I could finally roll over from my stomach to my side and breathe freely again, life surging into my body.

Awake and out of the fog, my mind cleared, and my heart opened. I had forgiven Scotty. And I had forgiven myself for not being the Christian woman I thought I was. I was still a Jesus-believing, Christ-following disciple of Jesus Christ. Even though I failed in some areas, Jesus still loved me and waited for me to turn to Him to acknowledge my mistrust and lack of faith.

Just like loving parents still love their rebellious, disobedient children and don't disown them because they are disobedient and rebellious. God did not disown me. Jehovah is a much more loving and patient Father. He understood what I was going through. Yahweh also knew I would return to Him in faith because of my love for Him. God understood I had head faith and not heart faith and lovingly waited for my head faith to align with my heart faith.

Marvelously, after Scotty was out of the house, I started dreaming pleasant, beautiful, serene illusions, all in total contrast to the visions seen when living with Scotty. My new images were themes of prosperity and happiness, just as genuine as nightmares, but I awoke with peace and joy.

One of the dreams showed me owning a beautiful, grand, white, two-story, 25,000-square-foot home. Gorgeous, plush, green grass, trees, and shrubs covered the landscape as far as my eyes could scan – north, south, east, and west. In the dream, I sat on a large, white fence, talking and rubbing the manes of my regal white, black, and brownish-red stallions, enjoying the peace and freedom of my surroundings. Everything on the property was pearl white – the home, fence, corral, sheds, storage areas, and guest cottages. With my hands waving, I awoke from the dream, thanking God for my freedom, peace, joy, and happiness. I then asked Jehovah to reveal if the vision meant anything.

A few nights later, I dreamt of owning another beautiful white mansion. This house was double the size of the previous dream house, at least 50,000 square feet. Again, everything was pearl white or white trimmed with pure gold. The magnificent home, Rolls-Royce, circular drive, guest cottages, and patio furniture were all white and trimmed with gold. Even the pool was white. Everything inside the house was also white and gold – furniture, carpeting, stairways, and walls. The doors and door posts were pure gold, but everything else was a vibrant white.

When I strolled through the kitchen, the stainless-steel pots and pans sparkled silver-like as they hung on the massive wall. Fresh-cut flowers deodorized every room, the deck, and the tables near the pool. Several people came to serve me as I sat at a table near the pool.

I awoke smiling. "What does this dream mean, Lord? White symbolizes holiness, purity, righteousness, and innocence, and gold symbolizes endurance, honor, and value. I've also heard that gold symbolizes being refined and going through the fire."

Although I beseeched Yahweh for days for a meaning to the dreams, I didn't receive a revelation. But it was a much better experience dreaming of peace, joy, happiness, and prosperity than snakes and being beaten unconscious.

·❤·❤·❤·❤·❤·

After the separation, it took months of Christian counseling and seeking a deeper relationship with Jesus before I felt like my usual self again. Scotty had infected my spirit more than I ever thought possible.

Dr. Joyce was the most wonderful Psychiatrist any lady could have had. She was patient, listened, prayed before and during our sessions, gave on-target insight, *and* was a Christian. She helped me realize Satan set me up from the beginning. He recognized a haughty, over-confident spirit of religion in me and used it to try to destroy me.

My therapy sessions had started six months into my tumultuous marriage. By the end of our union, Scotty had torn me into fragments, and it took creativity and patience to sew me back together. After many analysis sessions and multiple affirmations, Dr. Joyce said, "Hannah, it's time for you to get pushed out of the nest. You're strong enough to fly on your own." She sandwiched my hands between hers, smiling with her eyes and mouth. "You have improved tremendously since we first met, Hannah, and have gained helpful insight into most of your issues."

My breath quickened, and I nibbled my bottom lip.

She released my hands, leaned back into her chair, rested her chin on her hand, and gazed down. She looked up. "The answers usually lie within the individual; you just need to ask the right questions." A broad smile crossed her face again, and her eyes and nose crinkled. "I'm not cutting the umbilical cord, just extending it a bit to allow you to handle situations independently." She paused. "I will only be a phone call away and will squeeze you in any time."

A loud exhale slipped through my lips. "I appreciate all you've done for me, Dr. Joyce." My shoulders slumped, and Dr. Joyce raised her chin and lifted her right hand, reminding me to lift my head and push my shoulders back.

"Thank you for helping me feel good about myself again."

She tapped my hand. "You were always royalty. You just forgot who you are. But you're back and stronger from the trial."

A heavy sigh came, and my head bowed, but I quickly straightened my back and lifted my head. "I am through with men: old, young, and in-between. I have bad luck with husbands. I've tried it twice and failed...." My voice stammered, and no more words came.

Dr. Joyce looked at me with furrowed brows, her fingers steepled underneath her chin.

My face reddened, and my words stuttered, "It's going to take practice for me to stop saying I failed. I've tried it twice, and it didn't work out." My lips twisted. "Some people aren't meant to be married. Maybe I'm one of those people. I'll focus on getting closer to the Lord and making Him my husband."

Dr. Joyce's head nodded. "Focusing on the Lord and making Him your husband is a noble choice. But, I would like to encourage you not to give up totally on men simply because you chose unwisely twice. It may be that once you've made God your husband and is totally and completely surrendered to him, He may allow your godly mate to find you. Remember that Proverbs 18:22 (NKJV) says,

> *"He who finds a wife finds a good thing, and obtains favor from the Lord.""*

As we strolled to the door, Dr. Joyce said, "I'm going to share some wisdom that a friend gave me before I married. If you should meet a man sold out to the Father, Son, and Holy Ghost, and is also married to Christ, as you will be, don't be impressed by what he says but by how he lives. A tree is known by the fruit it bears – watch what type of fruit his life produces." She stopped at the door but didn't open it.

She continued,

> *"Beware of false prophets, who come to you dressed up as sheep while underneath they are savage wolves. You will recognize them by their fruit. Can grapes be picked from briars, or figs from thistles? A good tree always yields sound fruit, and a poor tree bad fruit"* Matthew 7: 15-18 (REB).

"In other words, look out for wolves in sheep's clothing.

"Don't date for the sake of dating. Know what you want out of the relationship and discuss it with your potential mate – let him know that you don't date to have companionship but expect it to lead to marriage.

"Once you understand what each wants, don't spend time alone, especially at night. The lustful spirits come out at night. Try to plan dates where there will be many other people around." She lifted my chin and smiled. "That is if you're planning to remain celibate until marriage.

"Don't let him touch you in erogenous zones. Holding hands may be safe, but depending on the physical feelings aroused, you may need even to avoid holding hands. Remember that holding hands can lead to touching, touching to caressing, caressing to fondling, and rubbing to fornication." Her eyes hemmed mine.

My shoulders shrugged. "That's why I'd rather stay away from men. If I'm not dating, I don't have to worry about committing fornication."

Dr. Joyce's lips pressed together. "How can I say this differently?" She shifted her standing position. "I'm not saying that you will commit fornication if you date. The Holy Spirit will warn and protect you if you are genuinely submitted. There's a scripture that says,

> *"No temptation has overtaken you that is not common to man. God is faithful, and He will not let you be tempted beyond your strength, but with the temptation will also provide the way of escape, that you may be able to endure it" I Corinthians 10:13 (RSV).*

"Just because you date doesn't mean you will be tempted to fornicate. I'm reflecting on the issues you shared in the sessions and your guilt about sleeping with Scotty before you married. You didn't plan to sleep with him, but it happened. I'm just trying to give you a lifeline and a plan."

"Thank you. I will remember those tips. Don't date for fun. Don't let him touch me. Don't be alone with him. Be honest with him about my intentions."

Dr. Joyce nodded and held the door open.

My voice trembled. "I wonder how I'll react when I run into Scotty again. I haven't seen him since we divorced."

"You'll be fine, Hannah. You have a sweet, forgiving, godly spirit. I believe you have forgiven him, but only God knows. A scripture in Isaiah says,

"........whether you turn to the right or to the left, your ears will hear a voice behind you, saying, this is the way; walk in it" Isaiah 30:21 (NIV).

"If you continue to listen to Jehovah's voice, which is the Lord directing you, you will make the correct godly decisions."

Months later, my pulse and breath accelerated when I ran into Scotty at an outpatient medical clinic. I almost didn't recognize him. He was being pushed in a wheelchair by a caregiver and looked much older and frailer. My head said, "Turn and rush in the opposite direction or pretend that you don't notice him."

Remembering Dr. Joyce's affirmations, I gingerly strolled past him with sweaty palms, a racing pulse, and quickening breaths. Conscious *not* to pick up my pace, I looked into his eyes and smiled as the love of God flowed through me. "Hello, Scotty."

He nodded and bowed his head.

As I glanced at him in the wheelchair, a blanket across his lap, and an aide pushing him, my heart grieved for him. A white tube with a white bandage protruded from his neck, which I recognized as a trachea tube. *Why is the bandage around his head?* I wondered. He was rail thin and looked much older than his years.

My feet stuck to the tiled floor, and then I turned and watched the caregiver push Scotty onto the elevator. His greatest fear had become a reality – he was incapacitated and needed someone to care for him.

Tears filled my eye sockets as I shifted my feet and exited through the doors. I dabbed the water from the corners of my eyes that sneaked through. As I continued down the hall, overwhelmed with the joy of the Lord, I noticed that the palpitations and rapid breathing had flown away. No anxiety. No anger. My body felt relaxed like it was floating on a feather. I knew I was at peace.

Isaiah 54: 5-6 (REV) crossed my mind.

> *"For your husband is your maker; His name is the Lord of Hosts. He who is called God of all the earth, the Holy One of Israel, is your redeemer. The Lord has acknowledged you a wife again, once deserted and heart-broken; your God regards you as a wife still young, though you were once cast off."*

While I strolled through the exit doors, I wanted to laugh, jump, dance, and spin around like a child. Instead, a broad smile covered my face, and my arms swung as I sauntered with my chin up, shoulders squared, and my head high, *knowing* I had passed the test of unforgiveness and was finally FREE!

HANNAH'S WORDS OF WISDOM

If you should meet a man totally sold out to the Father, Son, and Holy Ghost and is married to Christ, as you will be, and Jesus is the head of his life, reflect on these words of wisdom before saying the words, "I do."

One - Don't be impressed by what he says but by how he lives. A tree is known by the fruit it bears – watch what type of fruit your partner produces in his life. *"Beware of false prophets, who come to you dressed up as sheep while underneath they are savage wolves. You will recognize them by their fruit. Can grapes be picked from briars, or figs from thistles? A good tree always yields sound fruit, and a poor tree bad fruit"* Matthew 7: 15-18 (REB).

Two – Don't date for the sake of dating. Know what you want from the relationship and discuss it with your potential mate. Let him know that you don't date to have companionship but expect it to lead to marriage.

Three – Once you both understand what each wants, don't spend time alone with him, especially at night. It seems that the lustful spirits come out at night.

Four - Try to plan dates when many people will be around.

Five – Don't let him touch you in erogenous zones. Holding hands may be safe, but depending on the aroused physical feelings, you may need to avoid holding hands. Remember that holding hands can lead to touching, caressing, rubbing, fondling, and then to fornication.

LEAVE A REVIEW

I would love to read what you thought of Wormwood Marriage. You can write a review with your thoughts at:

Amazon

Goodreads

Facebook

Connect with the author:

Website: www.bhcarterauthor.com

Instagram: www.instagram.com/bh_carterauthor

Twitter: www.twitter.com/bh_carterauthor

Facebook: www.facebook.com/BHCarterMinstry

Email: barbara@bhcarterauthor.com

SNEAK PEEK

Turn the page for a sneak peek at B H Carter's next novel.

UNEXPECTED COMPATIBILITY

Available fall-winter 2024

CHAPTER ONE

Driving along Highway 44 on her way home after visiting Aunt Lucy, the yellow, orange, and red sky reminded Bernadette of a Monet painting as the sun disappeared behind the trees. She enjoyed the tranquility, stunning scenery, and even the tweeting birds and croaking frogs.

Even after eight years, the roads were still familiar as she drove away from the town she had once called home. The merriment of her birthday celebrations that had brought her back had filled her with a little less dread than she expected.

The landscape changed when she turned off the freeway onto the tar-covered street, taking a shortcut through Sorek's Valley. A streak of light slit through the woods as the glowing, dying sun slipped away.

Without any apparent reason, a slight trembling started in her legs and traveled up through her body. The air thickened as if a fog had filled the vehicle, shortening her breath as she drove further into the Valley. Hidden behind a foggy film, the full moon slowed as the red PT cruiser rattled along the dirt track into the ravine.

As she descended the pothole-scattered path, her car bounced when her tire hit each hole. Twittering bird and gravelly frog sounds disappeared. A deadness jammed the atmosphere – the quietness was deafening.

"I don't remember the trail being this rough," she said as she swerved left, right, and left again, navigating the rocky and bumpy route.

Her head bobbed, and her body bounced as she went into the gorge. Bernadette's skin itched all over, a nervous reaction she often experienced whenever anxiety spiked. She wet her lips several times while chewing gum to lubricate her mouth. The blood-colored October sun had disappeared behind the trees, and the last rays of sunlight crept backward over the earth. Her breathing became strained as an invisible rope twisted tight around her chest. She inhaled deeply and rapidly, her breaths whistling. Diagnosed with pantophobia, the fear of everything, and low self-worth escorting it, she understood the panic. But this was a different feeling.

Bernadette Wilson, you should have obeyed the voice in your head telling you to stay on the highway.

When the aroma of a dead animal seeped into the car, she covered her nose in disgust. Her eyes squinted westward following the disappearing radiance of the sunset. Ominous shadows blanketed the Valley.

Bernadette spotted a man wearing blue jeans and a plaid shirt standing on the verge of a pond as she approached the end of the road. He appeared to come out of nowhere. He stared in her direction but looked beyond her, with one thumb in his jean pocket and the other arm hanging at his side. Weeping willows grieved into the lake behind him.

"Hello!" she yelled over the half-rolled-down window while u-turning. She cleared her throat as a cough threatened. "I didn't notice you when I drove up."

The man continued gazing but didn't reply.

The October wind whirled leaves into the air. She squeezed the blue parka around her neck and glanced around the dreary gulley.

"Um, this passageway doesn't go through anymore, huh?" she asked quietly, shyly.

The man tugged on the tail of his untucked shirt. "This path ends here. And it's the end of the road for you too."

Frowning, she whipped her head up. Grotesque shadows of different sizes and shapes surfaced. Green, red, brown, coral, yellow, and purple eyes without torsos shone in the twilight, glowing in the gray, dusk light. Black mist swirled from the eyes. Something vinegary and musky stung her nose. She coughed, the tang of rotten meat making her gag. Seconds later, her dinner spewed through the open window.

A cacophony of popping, cracking, and rattling sounds surrounded the vehicle. Bernadette looked in all directions. Hundreds of eyes bolted toward the car from behind trees, boulders, and out of the water. Her body started shaking.

Hands trembling and heart pounding, she looked around. The monstrous silhouettes transformed into men with crazed expressions, surrounding the car and throwing objects at the windows.

She watched the creatures encircle her vehicle, her heart ticking in rhythm with her wristwatch. Her heart rate increased, thumping like it was about to explode. She slid her trembling hands around the steering wheel, hit the accelerator, and the vehicle shot forward. She drove as fast as she could to get out of there.

Staring in the rearview mirror as she sped away, she watched in terror as the man in the plaid shirt shot at her with an unusual weapon.

His comrades shrieked unintelligible words as they chased her with outstretched arms.

BelaZaar towered at the summit of the Valley in his demonic body, orchestrating the scene before him. "I have monitored Bernadette Wilson since birth, preparing her to be a high priestess in Lucifer's kingdom." He growled.

"I put my plans in motion by guiding her to Lakeview, Arkansas, to see her family for her thirtieth birthday. I gave no order to attack! She was to *see* the demons only and afterward surrender to her destiny as Lucifer's property." He stared toward the stream and spotted Death pacing at the water's edge. "What is he doing here?" He glared. "My plan was angel-proof. The visitation in the Valley should have sealed the pact."

His fangs clenched, and the veins in his neck bulged.

"Why was Death there? I did not summon him." *I will deal with him at another time.*

He eyed Death as he hunched and paced. *My master gave Bernadette to me. I have plans for her to rule as a high priestess representing the next generation. What is my challenger, Death, doing here? He cannot have her. She belongs to me.*

Bernadette gasped. "Where did those ... men come from?" The PT cruiser lurched onto the winding dirt track at over one hundred miles an hour. Hands wet with sweat, eyes blurry with tears, she was deaf to the horn-blowing. She spotted the blue tractor too late as she lunged toward the roadway, unable to stop. A silent scream ricocheted inside her as she collided with the powerful vehicle.

The tractor propelled the PT cruiser into the air, and the car plunked back onto the blacktop, rolling over several times before landing in a ditch. The scent of fresh tar circled the air as Bernadette pushed against the jammed door briefly before she lost consciousness.

CHAPTER TWO

Chico Montanez hit the table with his fist after discovering the selling price changed before he could meet with the seller. His jaw clenched on the call as he attempted to negotiate. If this deal failed, he'd lose his status as the number one lawyer in the area. Forcing a smile while the veins throbbed in his neck, Chico finally convinced the landowner to accept the original selling price.

His climb to the top hadn't been easy since he was still considered an outsider in Mississippi. He had attended high school with his cousins, Alfresco and Hadeco Carrasco, in Los Angeles, followed them to Las Vegas after graduating from law school, and then to Tunica when the twins relocated.

After his Black/Mexican Christian twins presented Chico to their casino boss, Chico became his attorney. He drove straight over and gripped the client's hand tightly before handing over an expensive pen to sign the contract. His chin was up and shoulders squared. He gave a close-lipped smile as he took the signed contract, then asked for introductions to the other owners.

Moments later, a grin flashed across his lips when the pretty secretary handed over a list of names and phone numbers. His fingers gently slid across her hand when he took the information. He left the complex and slid in next to a tall, shapely colleague waiting for him in his Porsche Boxster. He was confident that he would be the sole representative for most of the gaming clubs within a month.

Chico dropped off his colleague and then drove to his cousins' home, where he ate dinner most evenings. Sitting in the same spot at their mahogany dining table, he dominated the conversation, washing the meal down with white wine. His eyes watered, and a cough sprung from his throat when a mouthful of food refused to go down. Chico cleared his throat, massaging his neck at the same time.

"Slow down, Cuz," Alfresco and Hadeco said simultaneously.

"Drink some water." Alfresco put a glass of water in Chico's hand.

"I'm okay, dudes. The meat just went down the wrong pipe." He flashed a smile. "Abuela phoned this morning; she told me you called and wanted to know why I never called." His lips tightened. "You fellows are making me look bad. Stop calling her every day."

The twins stared at Chico with flat expressions.

"How about just phoning her once a week, and I'll make it a point to call her monthly?"

"She prays with us every morning and would pray for you too if you called her," said Alfresco.

"Abuela understands that I'm busy with my practice, and I call her when I have–"

Hadeco interrupted. "She prays every day for you to accept Jesus, Chico."

"For Christ's sake, I was raised Catholic, just like everyone else."

"She wants you to trust Him, Chico," said Alfresco. "Abuela wants you to have a personal relationship with Jesus, not just hear about Him now and again."

Chico gazed at the twins with a blank look on his face, deciding whether to continue the conversation or not. He changed the subject: "I'll need you compañeros to sign those papers if you want to buy the land before someone else does." His eyes danced, forgetting the previous discussion. "I needed to call in some favors to keep it off the market for another week. You owe me, and I will collect." A slight smile slanted his lips.

"Don't try to play us, Chico," said Alfresco, his eyes and mouth smiling. "I think you forget who you're talking to, man."

"We don't owe you squat." Hadeco folded his arms across his chest and pretended to be irritated. "If anything, you're in our debt for letting you follow us to Vegas and Mississippi," he added, winking at Fresco.

"You must be out of your mind, Deco." Chico put more food in his mouth.

"And, cousin," Alfresco said with a grin as he held a fork full of asparagus in midair, "you are indebted to us for introducing you to our boss."

"You gemelos have been in the Mississippi sun too long." Chico faked anger and disappointment as he took a sip of wine. "It has fried your–"

Hadeco cut him off. "Man, you will forever be obligated to us." His expression was stern, but his eyes were jolly.

Alfresco added, "So, tell your new clients you need to call in some favors." Alfresco's brown eyes twinkled. "They wouldn't know any better and might believe you."

Chico laughed as he gulped the rest of his wine. "You dudes know that I do honest business."

"Yeah, you're good people, man," said Alfresco. "Show us where you want us to sign."

Hadeco added, "You're a bit too direct at times, but you get the job done."

Chico clasped his arms behind his body. "Let's go celebrate, primos." Laughing loudly, he headed toward the door.

DEDICATION

I devote this book to the source of my being and the great I AM, God; to my rock, shield, strength, and redeemer, Jesus Christ; and to my advocate, translator, and intervener, the Holy Spirit.

I commit this book to all women going through a storm, those who experienced chaos and survived, and to the ones who interceded for others in turmoil.

I devote this book to my mother, the late Estella Kincaid Harvey; to Darrin, Melody, Tarrin, Kameron, and Jaylen Carter; my son, daughter-in-law, and grandchildren; to my sisters, Estella Harvey Williams, Essie Harvey Clayton, Minister Joyce Harvey Davis; and Susie Harvey Davis and Elnora Harvey Wilson post mortem; to my brothers, Reverend Larry Harvey, Ira Harvey; and Reverend Nathaniel Harvey Jr., Willie H. Harvey, and Lonnie L. Harvey post mortem.

Lastly, this second book is dedicated to my nephew, Donald A. Wilson, who lovingly and tirelessly promoted my first novel, *Bedeviled*. It is also apportioned to all my family and friends who supported me in purchasing and promoting my first novel and encouraged me to write the sequel.

ACKNOWLEDGMENTS

I am grateful to my Heavenly Father for giving me the gift of writing, Jesus for stirring up my ability, and the Holy Spirit for using my hands to get what He wanted me to say on paper. I wish to acknowledge my sister, Joyce Davis, who was blatantly honest in giving me her constructive criticism. Thanks, sister. Your feedback helped me remember that God gave us a Spirit of excellence.

My niece, Carolyn Davis Jones, gave me valuable input to help keep the story flowing, and I appreciate you. I also want to thank my former pastors, Apostle Charles, and Prophetess Evon Green, for teaching and preaching holiness, purpose, and kingdom reigning.

Lastly, I acknowledge the readers of *Bedeviled*, who gave me honest feedback about Scotty and Hannah, which gave me the theme and plot for Wormwood Marriage. I pray that you enjoyed reading about Scotty's new escapades.

ABOUT THE AUTHOR

Barbara Harvey Carter is a retired registered nurse residing in Texas. She has spent more than two decades as an addiction counselor, group facilitator, trainer, and healthcare professional in the medical and mental health specialties. Having worked with domestic abuse clients in her professional career and experienced the assaults of abuse, Barbara is knowledgeable and empathetic to the needs of abused women.

She believes in women's empowerment and supporting females in their endeavors. She also promoted holistic health – mind, body, and soul – as co-owner of SB Fitness Health Club for several years.

Before relocating, she volunteered as an intercessor, encourager, teacher, and planner at religious, community, and professional organizations. Besides being a fiction Christian author who writes about relationships, the supernatural, and the paranormal, Barbara enjoys spending time with her Lord, Jesus Christ, her son, Darrin, daughter-in-love, Melody, grandchildren Tarrin, Kameron, Jaylen, and her extended family.